If You Believe in Mermaids... Don't Tell

To Ben –
with very best wishes –
Ann A. Philips

A. A. Philips

Note: *Hans Christian Andersen Fairy Tales* (Odense, Denmark: Flensted, 1956), Copyright 1951 by Flensteds Forlag, is the source of all quotations from H.C. Andersen's story "The Little Mermaid."

First published by Dog Ear Publishing
4010 W. 86th Street, Ste H
Indianapolis, IN 46268
www.dogearpublishing.net

ISBN: 978-159858-359-5

This book is printed on acid-free paper.

Printed in the United States of America

"***If You Believe in Mermaids...Don't Tell*** presents a welcome and courageous book that speaks out for young people to be true to who they are."

–Alex Sanchez,
author of *Rainbow Boys* and *So Hard to Say*

"Todd and his story completely drew me in. This book is a rare find ... a different kind of hero's journey. Experience the struggles and the courage of a boy who, despite many forces that would stop him, must find his own way of being true to himself."

–Phyllis Rothblatt, M.A.
marriage and family therapist

"I cared about Todd at once; his quiet sense of humor, his generous spirit, his struggle to hide his inner nature, and his subsequent anxiety and fear that he will be found out. I also admired his courage, as exemplified by his willingness to put himself at risk so that, at least temporarily, he can be the person he really is. Todd is "different," yes, but what comes across so strongly is how absolutely "normal" he is, sharing so many of the same hopes, dreams, impulses and shortcomings as every other kid. This is a refreshing look into the heart of a great kid who views the world through a slightly different lens than most, but who only needs the acceptance of those around him to be able to flourish."

– Kathleen Jeffrie Johnson, author of
Target, *Parallel Universe of Liars*, and *Gone*

"Read this brave book to understand the world of the 'gentle boy'. A.A. Philips peers acutely into the soul of a boy outside the confines of traditional masculinity, to reveal the joys and pains of growing up while feeling different. The protagonist identifies with mermaids, the haunting beings that embody the mystery of living in-between two worlds, and thus he finds a safe haven amid the struggles to remain true to himself."

–Edgardo Menvielle, M.D., child psychiatrist,
Children's National Medical Center

"Finally we have a story that disputes the myth that all boys fit one form of masculinity. ***If You Believe in Mermaids ... Don't Tell*** gives comfort to boys who thought they were alone and provides an instructive message for adults who care about strengthening self-esteem in children. A.A. Philips implies ways of parenting beyond merely accepting difference – a journey toward actively affirming and celebrating their child's precious gifts."

–Catherine Tuerk, M.A., R.N., C.S.
nurse psychotherapist

"I couldn't put this book down. Its message of self love and acceptance will strike a chord in all who read it."

–Sue Shanahan, artist

"This book on a sensitive subject meets a need felt by young teens as they sort themselves out from the pressures of conformity."

–Carlee Hallman, poet and author
of *Abide with Me*

For Every Todd

ACKNOWLEDGMENTS

My abundant thanks to fellow writers, colleagues and friends Carol Purcell, Carlee Hallman, Denise Britti, Mary Rose Janya, Amie Rose Rotruck, Marjory Bancroft, Stephanie Lawson, Alex Sanchez, Nina Nelson, Mimi Bolotin, Maureen Neumann, John Moore, Edgardo Menvielle, Catherine Tuerk, Phyllis Rothblatt, Marci Riseman and the entire parent group listserv.

And to those nearest: Ella, who voiced the *YES* beyond every *NO*; Ken, who embodies the pleasures and discipline of writing; Joel and Deb, who cajoled me into bringing the story to life.

Chapter One

On Saturday morning I wandered into the living room and saw Dad up on a ladder installing the ugly new ceiling lamp. It looked like a land mine.

"Todd? When do you start camp?" Dad asked.

"I just finished seventh grade yesterday," I told him.

The land mine was hanging crooked. My parents didn't order the light I liked, with the frosty glass shade flaring out like a lily.

"What about baseball camp? Aren't you registered?" Dad went on.

"Nope."

Dad twisted toward me dangerously. "What happened? You were supposed to sign up in P.E.!"

I steadied the ladder. "I don't even like baseball."

Dad frowned at the ceiling. "Then soccer," he growled, dropping a screw. "Find out when it starts."

I trapped the rolling screw and handed it up to him. "I got bribed to play soccer when I was eight. You gave me ten bucks."

"And you found out you can run, and you liked it."

"Wrong. Just because I can run doesn't mean I like soccer. I'm a diver – remember? I'm going to the pool this summer. I'll swim laps every day. Come watch, if you don't believe me."

Maybe Dad would swim with me…

Dad jabbed the screwdriver into the fixture and twisted it hard. "The point is the *team*! Being part of a team. You're alone, mooning around. Go where the kids are. You'll make friends."

"I don't want those friends." *And I bet Dad wouldn't swim with me.*

"Good grief," Dad groaned, climbing down the stepladder. "Where did your mom put those camp brochures?" He tossed the screwdriver onto the sofa and ruffled through the pile of mail on the living room table, sorting out the camp brochures. "You'll like it when you improve," he said. "You can do it. A boy needs to learn discipline. Be out with the guys. Jeez, you think my father ever gave me the chance to go to a sports camp?"

He saw my second semester report card and pulled it out. *Uh-Oh.* I reached for it.

Dad scowled. "Phys. Ed. …C. Are you kidding me?"

I tried to pull the paper away from him.

Dad hung on with both hands. "Let go. How do you get a C in P.E.? Did you hide in the locker room or something?"

"Dad! What about the A's?"

"Those are okay," he said, finally letting go. "It's a pretty easy school, isn't it? You don't spend much time studying."

"I worked for those grades," I said, staring at the big A's next to History and Spanish.

"The C proves my point. Sports camp." He shoved the brochures in my face. "Pick one of these camps. *Right now.*"

I grabbed the pile from him and stomped up to my room. Kicked the door shut, tossed the brochures on the floor, and fell onto my bed.

I finally got out of school, away from the idiots dogging me. Now I had to go to a worse pit ... sports camp. Kids screaming down the field to flatten me and get whatever ball away from me. Guys crazy to bang into each other, get slammed and slam the other guy. And the coaches yelling at you to run faster, run over the other kid, get in there, fight for it!!

Why does Dad force me to go?

I poked the brochures with my toe.

Kids shooting baskets, whacking baseballs, lunging at soccer balls, waving lacrosse sticks sneered at me from covers of the dismal choice of torture camps.

And … a frog. A frog?? And kids swimming in a lake. I stretched over the side of the bed to grab the last brochure. Carroll Valley Nature Camp.

> At CVNC, youngsters from 8 to 14 investigate natural processes in a peaceful setting. We take a hands-on approach to environmental studies. Campers will observe the life cycles of common local species at close hand in an atmosphere of fun and cooperative teamwork.

Not a sports camp! This was my only hope. I knew Dad.

Maybe I could even practice diving at their lake.

I rolled off my bed and took the brochure down to Dad. "This one. I'll go to this camp."

Dad read the description and ranted. "How did this one get into the pile? Nature camp? You don't even like science. Didn't you get a B?"

"You told me to choose one. I pick the nature camp."

Luckily when Mom came home she backed me up.

"Come on, Darren. As long as Todd is doing something active, does it really matter? He'll learn a lot."

"Not what *I* want him to learn," Dad grumbled. But he gave in.

That was close.

It's weird about Dad. I can tell he'd like a different kind of son. So I don't get what I want from him, and he doesn't get what he wants from me.

It hasn't always been like this. I remember good times, like when he taught me how to swim. He stood in the pool and I'd hurl myself at him, over and over. Each time he'd back up, until he couldn't catch me anymore. But I didn't care. I kept jumping. I knew when I plopped in he'd reach out to scoop me up and hug me tight.

I was four.

After that I told him some things I wish I could take back. You find out that telling doesn't always make things better. Some stuff you shouldn't say, even to your parents. Even if you're only six years old and don't understand anything.

"Daddy, on the inside I'm a princess."

Nope. Don't tell. It has to be your secret. All yours.

* * * * *

Day One of nature camp – my very own *Survivor* show. I had to meet a whole new group of kids. Go out and pretend. In my room with the door closed, I practiced the BOY WALK. Step ... slouch. Step... slouch. You roll onto the outside of your foot so you sway a little, but just in the shoulders, not the hips.

I dug out the Stone Cold Steve Austin tee shirt my Dad gave me hoping I'd get interested in wrestling. I put it on. It's not going to matter what I wear. Clothes won't save me.

Looking in the mirror, I messed up my hair. I could go Goth, like some of the eighth graders. Wear the black eye make-up and the purple and green hair. Stick a ring in my lip. Maybe that would help.

At least my arms and legs aren't so skinny anymore. I don't look like E.T. as much as I used to.

Mom poked her head in the door. "Time to go, hon," she said. "Don't you want to comb your hair for the first day of camp? … Come on, don't look so unhappy. It's going to be fun. When I was little I loved the woods. Our TV didn't get any reception in the mountains, and that was such a gift. We discovered our own imaginations."

For Mom, everything is a gift. But for me, meeting a new group of kids is not a gift. It's slow-dripping water torture.

Maybe it'll be mostly girls. I get along with girls. Or maybe kids who go to nature camp aren't as bad? But there's always at least one shiznit. That's my word for the kid who starts out giving you that up-and-down look. From there it gets worse.

I sighed, grabbed my backpack, and headed for the car.

Fifteen minutes later we drove along the creek and up to the Carroll Valley Nature Center.The head counselor, Twig, gathered us together and introduced everyone. Under his floppy hat a long blond ponytail curved down his back.

Most of the kids were much younger, but there were two girls and a taller guy about my age. The girl with the blond streaks seemed familiar. Where had I seen her before? I slouched and tried to look bored. The kids were all white except for two little guys who were eyeing each other. I always notice now, since Darnell told me what it's like to be the only black kid in a group. Soon they'll figure out that *I'm* really the one who's different. It should take about a day.

While Twig was explaining safety rules and the buddy system, I was watching the butterflies behind him. In the big patch of flowers a painted sign read "butterfly garden". Fat bushes hung with long purple blossoms. Fluttering around them were amazing butterflies – little white and yellow ones, bigger black and orange ones, even black and gold striped ones. More butterflies here than I'd ever seen anywhere.

"Remember, you and your bud stick together – like bark on a tree – and listen for two toots of the whistle! When you hear it, stand beside your buddy" the counselor barked as he passed out clipboards. "If one of you falls in the pond, your buddy has to get my attention right away or you could turn up dead as a mackerel." Twig divided us into teams of two. “Now we’ll head down to the pond to learn about frogs.”

Just my luck, I was teamed with the big kid. He had black hair and blue eyes like that famous singer. His yellow tee shirt said ‘So many girls, so little time.’ The two of us headed downhill toward the lake.

“Whatup?” I said, barely glancing at him. “That counselor talks weird.”

He laughed. “He’s from Maine. I’m Brad. How old are you?”

“13,” I said.

He gave me the up-and-down look. “I’m 14. What school do you go to?”

“Trask Middle. I’m going into Eighth.“

“I know the *Trash Puddle*,” he said. “That place smells like barf.”

I stuck my chin out. The school is old, but it’s still my school. Brad was looking me over. I tried to control my hands and legs, and not roll down the hill.

“So you’re into the Hollywood Blonde?”

I looked around. Did he mean the blond girl?

“I don’t really know her,” I said.

He snorted. “Not the babe you were checking out. The Hollywood Blonde. Rattlesnake. Ringmaster.” he looked at me like I was pathetic. He waved a thumb toward my shirt.

"Oh, right," I said. "Right."

Those must be Austin's other wrestling names. Maybe.

"You're not much of a WWE fan," Brad laughed.

My face burned.

He laughed again. "Come on," he said. "Let's find us some frogs. Stick with me, 'cause we can basically do what we want. I know these trails blindfolded."

At the bottom of the hill I stopped by the muddy pond. "That's the lake?"

"What?" Brad said.

"I can't dive in that," I muttered.

"Why would you want to?" Brad scoffed.

I kept quiet.

"What were you expecting, an Olympic pool? This is nature camp, remember?"

I stumbled along behind Brad circling the mud-hole, listening for croaks. We sneaked up on a couple of frogs and saw them jump into the water. Then Brad squatted down and scooped something up from the grass.

"Awright!"

"What'd you get?" I asked.

"Take a look." He opened his hands a tiny bit so I could look in. A little bumpy brown thing – a toad, I guess – looked at me.

Suddenly the two girls were there. Brad stared at the blond. "Hell-o-o."

She was wearing tight lavender shorts with a matching striped top and even had lipstick on. "Nature Camp Barbie" turned to me. "I know you. Todd … right? I'm Sylvie. Remember me? I babysat for your little sister a couple of times."

"Oh, yeah," I said. SEEL-vee was the way she said her name. She used to be a brunette. Now her hair was streaked blond and longer – with her bangs all over to one side. A really pretty girl.

She stared at me, so I said something lame. "You changed your hair."

Brad snorted. She smiled and touched the strand hanging onto her shoulder. "You're right. I did."

Brad dropped the toad at her feet. "Oops!"

Sylvie jumped back with a squeak. I managed not to yelp.

The toad hopped frantically into the tall grass by the pond.

Sylvie made a face. "Very funny."

The other girl watched the toad hop away. "Brilliant," she said.

Brad grinned. "Sorry."

"Todd, this is Olivia," said Sylvie, barely tipping her head toward the other girl.

"Hi," I said. The girl looked past me.

Olivia was shorter than the rest of us and had a long black braid down her back and thick, dusty glasses. She wore faded denim overalls with a lot of pockets and old purple sneakers with holes in the sides. She and Sylvie were two different species.

"About this project...," Sylvie groaned, looking at me.

"We'll help you out," Brad answered, leaning over to look at her clipboard. "What have you got so far?"

"We haven't found a frog yet, but we heard some – we think they were frogs – so we wrote that down," Sylvie said.

Olivia turned away, toward the grasses swaying in the wind beside the pond.

Suddenly we heard the whistle toot twice, and Brad, Sylvie, and I pointed to our buddies. Olivia ignored us. Twig and the younger kids were in a bunch over on the other side of the pond. Twig waved to us and nodded.

Sylvie pointed at Olivia's back and rolled her eyes.

Brad sat in the grass. "Come on." He motioned Sylvie to sit beside him. Olivia ignored him.

"Okay – frogs are reptiles, right?" Brad announced.

Sylvie and I nodded. Brad smirked. "Brainless," he said. "Frogs are amphibians. Didn't you guys take Science? They have wet skin, not scales. So put that down under 'observations,' 'four-legged green amphibian, wet skin, lives near water'."

I actually knew that about frogs but it was safer to play dumb. Sylvie and I scribbled on our clipboards while Olivia did nothing

"Then for 'defense' – hey, they're green! They're camouflaged. They blend in. But if a snake comes along ...," Brad's arm crawled the air. "...froggie jumps in and swims away."

"Ugh," Sylvie shivered. "Why do we care?"

Blend in. Just blend in, I was thinking. *Like a frog.*

"It's their fate," said Brad in a low tone, opening his blue eyes wide. "Just like Fate brought us together."

Sylvie leaned away. "Well, frogs are slimy and disgusting."

"Hey, girl – don't dis the frogs. One might turn out to be your prince," Brad said.

"As *if*," said Sylvie.

Brad grinned at me, then at Sylvie. "I see you're ready for the kiss. Lipstick and all." Sylvie got pinker. Olivia turned to stare at Brad like he was a rare specimen.

I leaned back on my elbows into the prickly grass while they went back and forth.

The tall grasses by the pond gleamed neon green – so bright, they hardly looked real. They were waving in the breeze, like dancers bowing and swaying and stretching. Bright blue dragonflies were lighting on the grasses, like friends with fairy wings come to perch on the dancers' shoulders. I wanted to show someone how beautiful the tiny fragile wings were. But I wouldn't dare.

A silvery tail flashed in the water. A fish jumping! Or maybe ... *a mermaid. A little one, just the size for this pond. She was trying to escape from some gross thing down in the weeds. A giant fish had her trapped in his jaws. Just her head and arms were poking out, her long brown hair flowing from his mouth.*

I dove under and pried his jaws apart. The mermaid struggled out and flashed away.

I strained to hold the monster's jaws apart. Help!

Then she was back, with two long sticks. We propped the ugly fish's mouth open so he couldn't bite us, and finally I let go. We swam away holding hands before he could shatter the poles with his mighty jaws.

Sylvie tapped my arm.

Cut it out, loser. Stay in control.

Chapter Two

Sylvie was staring. "Hey, did you hear me?"

I shook off the make-believe. "Hmmm? Where's Brad?"

"He went over to talk to Twig." She fanned herself with one hand. "I want to go inside. I'm melting."

If she just moved a few feet she'd be in the shade.

"Your little sister was really cute. How old is she now?"

I shrugged. "She's five, I think."

"Do you two get along?"

"Actually, we do."

"I remember the last time I was at your house, she wanted me to tell her a story, and it *had* to be about mermaids. I made something up - - I thought it was pretty good." Sylvie raised her eyebrows. "But she said that *your* mermaid stories were way better. So I said, 'why don't you tell me one of *his* stories?'" Sylvie laughed.

I forced a smile. *How do I keep Casey from blabbing?*

"Honestly, I never babysat for a kid who liked her brother so much."

"Well that was last year," I said. "We'll probably hate each other this summer. I have to take care of her every day after camp for the next two weeks."

I looked around. Olivia lay on her stomach on the bank of the pond about 20 feet away from us, her chin resting on her hands.

Sylvie motioned toward Olivia and whispered, "What is she doing?"

"I don't know," I whispered back, "staring into the water?"

"She is so weird! I'm staying away from her."

"Me, too." I hoped Olivia couldn't hear. Maybe she's just shy. Or maybe she saw something cool. If I looked at a flower someone always asked, 'What are you doing? What are you staring at?' If you're not a little kid, you're not supposed to stare at beautiful things. Boys aren't, anyway.

Brad came strolling over to us, his eyes shining. "Rock on! I'm in charge of you guys today."

Sylvie's face dropped. "What do you mean?"

"Finally I get something back for all the years I wasted here," Brad tossed his head back. "The other counselor's poison ivy spread down his throat, so he's not coming to work. Anyway I'm 14, old enough to be a junior counselor, and I've been a camper here since I was five. I'm practically family."

Sylvie rolled her eyes. "Oooh. I'm impressed."

"Cool," I said. "No counselor to tell us what to do." Inside I was cringing.

"Well can we go inside? Please?" Sylvie begged.

Brad looked down at Sylvie and rubbed his chin with one finger. "Hmmmm…"

Sylvie was getting exasperated. "Come on, Brad, I'm dying out here in the sun."

"Okay, how about we check out the exhibits?" Brad suggested. "Hey, what's your name – *Olive*? Come on, we're going inside."

Olivia slowly got up and followed us. As we headed up the hill, Brad waved to Twig and pointed to the center. Twig nodded.

Inside it was a lot cooler. We walked down the hall to the room called the Discovery Center. One side of the room was lined with tanks and mounted exhibits.

Along another wall big tables were covered with microscopes and measuring tools and nature books.

We poked our hands in the "What Is It – Fur, Feather, Bones?" boxes. We looked at the plaster casts of animals tracks and the wasp nest.

"This guy is called Boxo." Brad lifted a turtle out of a tank and tapped his head. Whsst! The turtle jerked his head back into his shell. Brad lightly pinched a leg and the turtle pulled them in, too. The bottom part of the shell had a hinge and the whole thing snapped up tight, safe from predators. I could use that skill.

I noticed big colorful posters showing local butterflies. Sylvie pointed. "I love that yellow and black one with the tiger stripes," she said. "Look at the long tail ...feathers... whatever." She giggled. "What are those for?"

Brad interrupted. "Butterflies *have* no purpose. What's the point of butterflies?"

Sylvie smiled at me.

"No point," I said.

Brad went over to the big tank "Snakes, now.... Snakes eat rats. That's a purpose. Come over here and see the pine snake."

A long snake was lying on bark mulch. Its pale gray skin was splotched with black markings. "What, they live in pine trees?" I asked Brad.

"Yeah, check your yard." Brad lifted the cover off the tank and put both hands down over the snake.

Is that true? Are these things in my yard?

"Ugly," I said. It wasn't. It was just scary.

I looked for Olivia. She was over at the big table, peering into a microscope. Like the three of us weren't really there.

Brad scooped up the snake. The snake waved its head and tail around.

Oh, man.

"If you put that snake on me, Brad, you are *dead*," Sylvie said.

"I'm just showing you. Look at the tongue."

The split tongue was flicking in and out. His eyes were shiny wet.

Sylvie pulled away. "It's going to bite me!"

"They don't bite with their tongues! Come on! It's smelling you. Put out your hand," Brad said.

Sylvie kept her hands behind her back. "Stop waving him around!"

"Todd's not scared. Here, Todd."

I froze as Brad brought the snake up to my arm. I felt the tongue flick once on my skin.

"Put a finger out and touch it." Brad had a good hold on the snake, so I forced myself to rub my finger over the tail. It was cool, glassy. I could even feel the tiny edges of his scales.

Brad lifted the snake. "Feel underneath."

The stomach scales were completely different, wide parallel bands like stairs. I rubbed underneath with my fingertips. The scales felt like plastic. The snake's muscle tensed beneath my fingers.

Then Brad dropped the snake onto my hand. I pulled back as the snake's tail thrashed in the air.

Sylvie gasped. "Brad! You jerk!"

Laughing, Brad scooped up the dangling tail.

Suddenly Olivia was there, glaring at Brad.

"It's okay. No big deal," I said.

Brad is a menace. Just like the guys at school. One minute they're okay, then they turn into the enemy. By the time I got home I was exhausted. The whole day was like that. Sylvie is semi-nice, I guess. But Brad – he might spring on me any time.

One person I'm not stressing over is Olivia. I think she's got her own problems.

* * * * *

Mom takes us out somewhere every week "to develop family cohesion," she says. Dad and I call it family coHERsion. I wouldn't mind it if we actually had fun, but it never works out that way. Tonight we went to shop and have dinner at the mall, but the family was not even together. Mom bought me some shorts for camp while Dad looked at a new kind of gutter. Then Mom wanted to look for clothes for Casey in the little girl's section

I used to love going in there. I remember persuading little Casey to try on a pile of silky skirts and velvet dresses, when I was younger. Shopping took forever, so Mom stopped taking me along. She shopped with Casey while I was at school. I soon wised up and pretended I didn't care.

"Mom, I'm going up to Kay-Bee Toys while you shop for Casey," I said. "I don't want to hang around here."

"All right, but meet me outside by the escalator in 15 minutes. And don't lose that bag with your new clothes in it!" she called to me.

"Of course I won't."

I ran up to the upper level and into the toy store. I had seventeen dollars saved up. I haven't been in here for so long. I wandered up the model car aisle and the remote-controlled toy aisle, into the action figure aisles. I liked the action figures with lots of accessories – wings and capes and spears you can launch. There were thousands of monster guys and heroes for sale – a few girl figures, too. In first and second grade sometimes I'd find a little Princess Padma or Lara Croft on the playground, and I'd grab it and take it home. But eventually Mom always saw them and made them disappear.

Here was my chance to visit the forbidden land. Slowly I made my way down to the doll aisle. It made Mom irritated to see me there, even when I pretended I was just showing them to Casey. No friggin' way would they ever buy me a doll when *I* was little.

This whole long aisle was all Barbie – dolls, clothes, cars, furniture, everything. The Barbies with the long ball gowns were my favorites.

Whap! A greasy-haired clerk dropped a stack of Barbie boxes on the floor right by me. Then he gave me the look, like 'What are *you* doing in the Barbie aisle?'

"...I don't know which one she wants..." I muttered, all exasperated.

The clerk took his time arranging the boxes on a shelf, glancing at me out the side of his dirty glasses. Freaky-looking guy. Like the ones that shoot up schools for revenge.

"Forget this," I said and stalked off around the corner. I hung out by the paint sets till he was gone. Only three minutes left to look.

What if I *bought* one? Not to play with. Just to *do it*. All those years when I really wanted one, I was a helpless little kid ... I couldn't do anything about it.

I peeked again and the clerk was gone. I raced down the aisle and grabbed the brunette Prom Queen Barbie in the dark blue gown. Should I? *Should I?*

I walked toward the front of the store, the box pressed to my chest. As soon as I paid, I'd dump the box in the trash. Hide the doll in the bag with my new shorts. *Yes or No? I can't decide!*

A familiar voice floated up from the next aisle. "Hello Leila, how are you? Have you seen Todd?"

My mother is here! She can't find out!

I jammed the box into my Penney's bag as Mom appeared in front of me at the end of the aisle, holding Casey by the hand.

"There you are, Todd. Come on, it's time to meet Dad."

Oh, no.

I followed her like a puppy right up to the doorway. The alarm's going to ring. It'll be stealing. They'll call the police.

I started to throw my bag on the floor. But Mom was glancing back at me.

I'm Dead.

My shoulders hunched against the clanging in my ears. But no one came ... no one looked. I slunk out of the store. A cop was leaning over the second story railing, looking down. He didn't turn around.

The ringing sound was just in my head. *What happened? Why didn't the alarm ring?*

They have ways to catch you if you steal. I know they do. There are cameras all over.

Maybe they were watching me now.

We rode down the escalator and met Dad. He was buying something at a stand.

I tried not to look for the cameras. Security must be following to see if I steal anything else.

"Where do you and Casey want to eat?" Mom asked.

Another cop walked toward us. Here it comes. Mom and Dad will never forgive me.

"Todd? What's your vote?" Dad said.

The cop looked right at me.

"Todd?"

I clutched the bag. "I don't care."

"You make it sound like a punishment," Mom said.

Now the two cops were meeting up and talking. They looked around.

The bag was like a grenade in my hand. I should tell them all, right now. But if I do, Dad will see the doll. That can't happen.

"I don't want to stay for dinner. Let's go home," I said, looking for an exit.

"Could you try to give a little here?" Dad said, nudging me with his arm. "What's with you? You can't have dinner out with the family?"

If he knew what was in the bag ... if he knew I stole what was in the bag...

"He's not even paying attention," Mom said.

Casey pouted. "I want to go to Noodle-O's!"

"Overnight you're the obnoxious teenager," Dad said to me. "You and your attitude are not going to ruin our dinner. You can wait for us in the car."

Mom dug a tissue out of her pocket. "A trip to the mall and dinner. Is it really too much to expect?"

Dad handed me the car keys. Mom blew her nose. "Will he be safe?"

Dad put his arm around Mom. "The lot is patrolled. He'll be fine." He took Casey's hand and steered them away. "Come on, let's go have dinner."

Casey frowned back at me. "Why doesn't Todd come? Why is he mad?"

"In ten years, you'll understand," Dad told her.

I stayed there trembling while they walked away. *At least when I'm arrested I'll be alone. I won't see the look on Dad's face.*

I waited for a long time. Then I walked to the closest exit.

It took me half an hour to find the car.

Chapter Three

Why do people steal? Doesn't it make them crazy? Back home in my room I still had goose bumps. At every little noise I'd tiptoe over to listen at the door. Where do I hide her? Under the bed? Behind the games in the top of the closet? Behind the bookcase? Finally I stuck her under my mattress. But it felt like I had "*Doll*" tattooed onto my forehead. Any minute my family plus a TV newswoman were going to burst in and sniff out the doll hidden in the boy's room.

And what about tomorrow, when I'll be away at camp? And the days after that? She couldn't stay. I knew that. I should be happy, finally. But I wasn't.

I lay on my bed trying to relax.

I needed time.

A day at home, at least. Without camp. Without Brad.

Maybe Casey could help ....

After Dad said goodnight to her, I went into Casey's room to make her sick.

"If you don't feel good tomorrow, I'll probably have to stay home and take care of you," I told her. "I'll play with you all day. I promise."

Her eyes got big.

"But Mommy knows when I'm sick."

"It'll work. Trust me. You groan like this – *unnnhhh* – and say you feel bad. They'll believe you. Tell them your tummy hurts. Don't say anything else. Okay?"

"Okay. Will you watch Little Mermaid with me?"

"Sure, no problem."

When my alarm rang the next morning, I hustled into Casey's room to remind her to start moaning. Mom and Dad went to her and I heard them talking over their options. Then they called me in to say I should stay home with her.

I made a face. "Stay home all day?"

"I'm sure it's a 24-hour bug," Mom said, "and I really need to go to work today if I can. So does Dad. Hopefully she'll be better tomorrow."

Tomorrow, I'll have to find Barbie another home.

As soon as we were alone, Casey settled into the sofa in the family room to watch *The Little Mermaid.* I love that movie, but I won't get this chance again. Casey didn't need me. I hurried up to my room, dug out Prom Queen Barbie from under the mattress, whisked her into the bathroom and locked the door.

I can be with her one time. Just once.

I felt her satiny dress, the lacey sleeves, and the tiny necklace around her neck. I combed her long brown hair. I sat her in different positions on the sink cabinet, and dampened her hair to see how that changed the way it moved as she swayed and twirled. I pulled out the hair dryer and dried it, curling it under my fingers. Then I slipped over to my room to get my radio and a piece of rope. I turned the radio to the oldies station, knotted the rope to make a swing seat, and nestled Barbie in. Holding the ends, I swung her back and forth.

First the tide ... rushes in, plants a kiss on the shore, then rolls out to the sea...

I imagined her and me on giant swings in a magical playground.

So I'm crazy. So shoot me.

There was a soft green lawn. And when we swung, leaning back, our long hair swept across the grass.

And the sea ... is very still once more. So I rush ... to your arms...

I'll be crazy this once.

We swooped forward, up and up, all parallel and in rhythm, toes pointed toward the sky. Then the swings reached their peak and we fell back, hair flying and dresses billowing up around us. We sank down, down, pumping our heels back underneath us, leaning forward as our toes brushed the tall grass. The swings flew back and up till we hung in the air for an instant, nearly falling out, then we threw our shoulders back and our legs out before us, ready to drop again. And our hair hung in the air, waiting for us.

There she goes, just awalkin' down the street, singing doowah diddie diddie dum deedee do…

I took Barbie out of her swing and twirled her. The prom skirt flared out like an open umbrella and when she stopped, it twisted around her legs.

We were Cinderella and Princess Aurora. We were dancing for the royals and all the courtiers. We leaped and twirled and curtseyed. The dresses billowed up around us. We slid sideways back and forth, reaching and bending.

She looks good, she looks fine, and we're happy all the time…

RAP, RAP, RAP. Somebody knocked.

"Todd!" Casey yelled, right outside the door.

"What?"

"Do you have mon-ey?" she sang.

"Why do you want money?"

"For the man."

"Huh? Some guy in the movie is asking for money?"

"Not in the movie."

My scalp tingled.

"What guy? Where is he?" I croaked, shoving Barbie deep under the towels in the cupboard. I fumbled with the knob and unlocked the door.

Casey was alone in the hall.

"Where is he?"

"At the *door*," she whined.

"You let him in?!" I peered down the stairs. The front door was wide open.

"I yelled for you and you didn't come!"

"Shhhh! I didn't hear you calling me!" I tiptoed down and peeked around the door. Nobody there. I checked the front porch.

"There he is!" Casey pointed. A skinny guy hunched over a rickety bike was pedaling out the driveway and into the street.

"You opened the door? What are you, nuts?" I slammed it shut and locked it. "Who was he? What did he say?"

"He needs gas ... for his car. Give him some money."

"You can't let strangers into the house! You can't give them our money."

"Why?"

"He might ... st- steal our stuff," I stuttered. "Casey, don't talk to some stranger that shows up here!"

Her face crumpled. "You're my babysitter," Casey sniffled. "You're supposed to come and tell people."

"I would've if you'd come to get me! You opened the door right up to that weirdo? Don't you know any better?"

Casey started to cry. "You didn't play with me! You promised!" She ran up the stairs whimpering and disappeared down the hall.

"Hey, hey – you wanted to watch the movie!" I yelled after her.

"Anyway, that's not the point," I muttered to the wall.

My legs went weak and I slumped down on the stair.

What was the guy after? What if he'd grabbed her? Maybe I wouldn't have heard her scream. If she had time to scream.

My stomach flipped over.

After I imagined the worst for awhile, I climbed the stairs and went into her room.

She was lying on her rug with her arm over her face.

"Okay. Forget about it. It's over. Look, Casey, I'll play with you. Right now."

She lay still.

"Case, I'm sorry." I nudged her foot. "I'll do whatever you want. How about cards?"

Casey rolled onto her side and pulled up her knees, eyes still closed. Her long light hair was twisted around her neck. I wanted to loosen it for her, make her more comfortable. But she didn't seem to want to be touched.

"No, no, no," she said into the rug. "Go away."

I wanted to bring her back. Make her forget about the guy.

Could we play dolls? *No.* I stopped doing that with her a long time ago. I never knew when she'd mention it to Mom and Dad.

Ooops, I left Barbie in the bathroom. Right in the closet.

"I'll be right back, okay? I'll read you a story."

She was quiet.

On the way to the bathroom I tripped over my clarinet case I'd left in the hall. Hmmm .... Pulled Barbie out of the bathroom closet. Her dress was wrinkled from the weight of the towels. I smoothed it down, measured her beside the clarinet case, opened it, took out the clarinet, and tucked her in instead. Perfect fit.

Now, a story for Casey. Maybe *The Little Mermaid.* We had it somewhere in a fairy tale book.

It took me awhile, but I found the old dusty *H. C. Andersen Fairy Tales* up in the top corner of the bookshelf. Nobody had opened it for so long that the pages were stuck together, and they made a crackling noise when I turned them.

Back up in Casey's room, she hadn't moved. I sat down next to her on her rug.

"I'm going to read the real *Little Mermaid* story to you, Case," I said. "The one they made the movie from."

Not a peep. So I started in.

> **"Far out at sea the water's as blue as the petals of the loveliest cornflower, and as clear as the purest glass; but it's very deep, deeper than any anchor can reach .... Right down there live the sea people."**

I read about the sea King's palace, with walls of orange coral and long pointed windows of golden amber, a roof of purple cockleshells that open with the current to show a dazzling pearl in each one.

That's where I want to live.

When I glanced over, Casey's eyes were open.

"Tell about the mermaids," she whispered.

So I read about the widower sea King and the six pretty little sea Princesses.

> **"... the youngest was the loveliest of them all. Her skin was as clear and delicate as a rose-leaf, her eyes were as blue as the deepest lake."**

"You make the castle," Casey interrupted, sitting up. She was hooked. "And my dolls can be the mermaids. But they need tails!"

Oops. Dolls again. Mom and Dad will go green .... But Casey's sick. I have to do what she wants.

She dug out her dolls and we made tails from green paper and tied them on with ribbon.

Then I read how the old grandmother told the princesses that each one would be allowed to rise to the surface when she was fifteen to peek at the ships and towns and people. The oldest princess could go exploring, but the littlest princess had to wait five whole years.

Casey dug in her closet for more scenery for the sisters' visits up to earth and I thumbed through the pages. This was good. She'd forget to tell Mom I abandoned her this morning.

Later in the story Grandmother warns the Little Mermaid that a human wouldn't fall in love with a mermaid.

> **"The very thing that's so beautiful here in the sea, your fish's tail, seems ugly to people on the earth..."**

Uh-unh. If I could be a mermaid, I'd never give up my tail for anything. I'd know it was beautiful, even if everybody else thought I was wrong. Like they already do, anyway.

I found the end, and started looking for the scene where she marries the prince.

> **She saw the Prince with his pretty bride looking about for her; sorrowfully they stared at the heaving foam, as if they knew she had thrown herself into the waves...**

Wait! The prince marries somebody else? He's supposed to marry the Little Mermaid ... and they live happily ever after!

I flipped back a couple of pages. Early that morning her sisters brought her a knife and told her:

> **"Make haste! Either he or you must die before the sun rises."**

Casey is going to hate this. She wants to hear about the big wedding. Little M. has to get the prince … and she can't die!

Casey came back in with more props. "You be the Prince and the sea King," she directed. So my prince moped around on shore, waiting for the perfect girl, while each princess turned 15 and went up to the surface and had adventures. But I'm really worried about how this story is going to end.

Later, when it was time for Mom and Dad to be getting back, I warned Casey, "Let me talk to them." I saw her head nod from behind a big picture book. So I went downstairs.

"Hey Todd, How did the day go?" Dad asked, carrying in bags of groceries. Mom was right behind him with more bags.

"Okay."

"How is Casey feeling? I'm going right up to see her." Mom pointed to the bag on the table. "Would you put these in the freezer?"

"She's better. But just so you know, some guy came to the door while I was in the bathroom."

"What did he want?" Dad plunked the bags on the counter and started unpacking them.

"He wanted gas money for his car. That's what he said, anyway. Casey opened the door."

Dad swung around to look at me, one hand still down in the paper bag.

Mom held out the frozen peas. "*WHAT?*"

"Please don't yell at her, okay? 'Cause I already did."

Dad's face went grim. "Just tell us what happened."

"Casey went to the door … and I was in the bathroom, so I didn't hear the knock, and then she came to get me."

"*And?"* Mom edged toward the door, pressing the bag of frozen peas to her chest.

"And I go downstairs quick and the guy is riding away on a bike …"

"On a bike?" Dad was confused. "I thought he wanted money for his car."

"I know. Anyway, I locked the door and I told Casey never, ever to open it."

Mom and Dad looked at each other. I could see them sifting through the possibilities in their minds.

"Is she okay? Where is she?" Mom threw the peas in my direction and rushed to the door. The bag splatted open on the floor. Four hundred and seventeen peas rolled out.

I squatted to chase them down. "Mom. She's fine! Don't be mad at her, okay? It was nobody's fault."

"Darren, just think!" And Mom was gone.

"Did he come back? Did you see him again? Did you get a good look at him?" Dad asked, staring at me. He didn't pick up one pea.

"Nope and nope." I scooped peas into the bottom of my tee shirt and looked around for something to put them in.

"Unbelievable." Dad pressed one palm against his forehead. "Unbelievable."

I found a plastic bag, emptied the peas in, and tossed it into the freezer.

"Why is it unbelievable? Nothing happened."

Dad jerked the milk containers out of the bag and jammed them into the refrigerator.

"She was at the door... completely vulnerable... and where were *you?* It wasn't even locked!"

"Dad ...,"

"SHHH!"

Casey came running in and jumped into his outstretched arms. "Daddy!" They hugged.

"A bad man came here to take our money," she said with big eyes.

Mom and Dad shot me evil looks.

"Maybe he did need help," Dad said, squeezing her. "But a grownup needs to deal with people who come to the house. It's better if Todd doesn't open the door either, unless it's a real close friend."

"That's right," Mom chimed in. "Keep the door locked. Don't answer if someone knocks. Haven't we told Todd this before?"

"Of course we have. But maybe we should print a sign for the inside of the door that says 'Do Not Open', as a reminder to both of them."

"I can help," chirped Casey. "I can make 'A'.

Dad patted her on the head. "Attagirl. First let's get dinner going. I'm starving."

After dinner and another lecture I took the fairy tale book with me, locked my door, and read the whole mermaid story through.

The ending sucked big time. In fact, the whole story was depressing. First she had to wait five long years to go up to the surface, then when she got her legs every step was awful pain, and at the end she died and turned into foam on the water. Goody.

"Todd!" Mom yelled from the hall. "What is your *clarinet* doing in the bathroom? Where is the case?"

Chapter Four

On the way out of our neighborhood the next morning I caught a glimpse of a guy swerving around a corner on his bike. Was it the same guy? Nah – this one was in biker shorts. And maybe the man at our door did need money. Lost his job or something. It could be.

At camp Brad charged right over to me "Where were you yesterday? Did you hear we're going to the lake? Did you bring your suit?"

"To swim in the mudhole?" I said. "Great."

"Nah. We're walking over to Bennett Lake. It's just through the woods."

Twig led us down the trail toward the big lake nearby. I walked behind Sylvie, her swatting at gnats the whole way. Brad talked, but I didn't hear much. I pictured hiding Barbie in the woods, under the leaves. I don't want to stick her in the dirt, but Mom and Dad could find her anytime, like they almost did last night.

I didn't have my suit, but my shorts would do. I don't like undressing in front of people anyway. While the others were changing in the locker room, I stashed my shirt in my backpack and went onto the beach. Finally – a real lake to swim in!

Twig stood waiting for the kids to come out. "Todd – I'd like you to buddy with Olivia. She may not swim, but check on her now and then."

I groaned "Okay" as I walked into the water.

It felt cool just for a few seconds, then silky and soft flowing across my skin. I swam out to the raft. It was still early, so hardly anybody was around. Two lifeguards sat on raised chairs, one at each end of the beach.

I'm an okay diver. I taught myself, from the video I got at the library last year. Practiced almost every day at the neighborhood pool, and by the end of the summer I felt like a diver. Someday I'll do the one-and-a-half somersault. But when I don't have a board, the backward dive is my favorite. I stretched straight-legged to touch my toes a couple of times, then backed up to the end of the raft, my feet halfway over the edge. Dropped my heels, lifted my arms, circled them down and up, and jumped back, arcing arms and body toward the water. Sky, trees, water flashed by upside down. No zip entry, no vertical, but not bad. Leaping back blind feels scary. But I'm in control.

"Dude, you're a diver?" Brad said as he swam over.

"Sort of," I said. "Let's see your jackknife."

"Hah! Let's see *yours*," he answered.

"You would, but there's no board here," I said.

And there was Sylvie on the shore in a bright pink two-piece, shading her eyes from the sun as she looked around.

"Sylvie! Out here! Come on!" Brad shouted to her. Sylvie waved and tiptoed into the water hunching her shoulders as if it was cold. I was glad to see her coming. Too much time with Brad isn't good for my health.

I looked up and down the beach for Olivia. Finally I spotted somebody short, way down at the end, leaning over some tall reeds. That had to be her. Probably happy as a clam, like Twig says.

Sylvie was doggy paddling all the way out to the raft, her neck stiff above the water. I bet she was trying to keep her hair dry.

She struggled up the ladder and lay down on the warm boards. "There's all that yuck on the bottom. Did you feel it?"

"Don't put your feet down," Brad told her. "This is nature, Syl."

Sylvie had hot-pink nail polish to match her suit, and her hair held up with a pink and gold scrunchie.

"I don't want nature. I want a cement swimming pool with plenty of lounge chairs and cold cokes at the concession stand," she said, shielding her face with the crook of her elbow. "What have they got here? Anything?"

I looked around for a food stand and didn't see one. "Gatorade and granola bars," I said. They both groaned.

Brad stood looking at Sylvie's curvy body. It was pretty attractive. Finally she looked up.

"Brad. *Enough.*"

He grinned. "Come on – dive contest."

"You go ahead," she yawned, pulling the scrunchie out and shaking her hair loose. "I'll watch."

We took turns with front and back dives. Brad can do a decent front dive, but he's got no style.

"Sorry Brad," Sylvie teased. "Todd is just better."

If I had a board here, my tuck and layout would totally humiliate him.

Brad was getting pissed. "Yeah, Todd's one of the *pretty* divers."

Ooops. Time to disappear.

I dove in fast and this time I swam to shore and walked to where Olivia sat by herself, examining leaves. She was wearing some loose faded shorts and a big plaid shirt.

"Hey," I said. "What's up?"

She glanced up. "Yes?"

"So ... are you going to swim?"

"I don't know," she said, her voice strained.

"We're on the raft. Come out if you want."

Her eyes flickered toward me but her face was toward the lake. "Maybe later."

"Okay. See you," I said, and walked away. Well, I got told.

As I climbed back up on the raft, Sylvie sat up. "What did you say to Olivia?"

"Why is Twig making *me* watch over her? Why not one of the little shizbrat nature-lovers?"

That got a laugh from both of them.

"Shizbrats? I like that. Listen, Olivia's demented," Sylvie sighed.

"You mean *retarded*," Brad interrupted.

Sylvie grinned at him. "Whatever. Anyway she doesn't appreciate Todd or you."

Brad tugged on her arm. "Come on. Forget her. Let's see you dive."

"No, I'm watching," Sylvie insisted. Brad pulled her up off the boards.

"Brad!" she yelped, pulling back.

It's because of her hair, I thought. Or maybe she likes lying on the raft being looked at.

A long shrill whistle blew. "Knock off the horseplay on the raft!" the lifeguard yelled. Everybody on the shore turned to stare at us.

Brad dropped Sylvie's arm and she plopped back down.

"Nazi," Brad muttered.

Twig walked to the edge of the water closest to the raft and pointed at us.

"We'll be good! We promise!" Brad sang out to him. Twig nodded.

I noticed a dark head in the water. Olivia. She was treading water ten feet from the raft.

"Oh great. Thanks, Todd. Here comes the dark cloud," Sylvie murmured.

Did I invite her out here? My mistake. Why do I worry over every lost person? Now I have to fake cool – for Sylvie and Brad. Pretend I'm not a boy with a stolen doll in my room.

The raft tilted with the new weight as Olivia climbed up the ladder. She had a dark blue one-piece suit on, so loose and stretched-out that it wrinkled over her round stomach. Maybe it was her mother's. Maybe her grandmother's. This girl needed help. Sylvie clamped her lips together and smirked at me.

"Hi, Olivia," she said, super-brightly. "Are you going to dive? These guys are good. Especially Todd." She wrinkled her nose at Brad.

Olivia glanced around, but barely seemed to focus without her glasses. She walked to the edge and looked over. Then she fell in sideways, her legs all crooked.

Whoa!

"What was *that*?" Brad said.

"Forward dive with a half twist, minus the dive," I said.

Sylvie's head rolled back. "Oh my gosh – that suit!" she cackled.

"Salvation Army reject," I said.

"Now I feel sorry for her," Sylvie purred. "I might even give her a makeover. Should I, Todd?"

"Without those big glasses, at least you could see her eyes," I answered. "They might even be pretty with some makeup."

"Huh?!" Brad snorted. Oops again.

Olivia hadn't come up yet. "Where'd she go?" I said.

"You can tell by the wrinkly skin – she's part frog. She's fine," Brad said.

I looked around.

"Brad."

"What?"

"She didn't come up! I'm supposed to check on her...."

"She dissed us to hook up with another neutered frog."

The sun was behind a cloud and I couldn't see anything under the surface, so I slid off the raft and dove under near the spot where she'd gone in. The water was murky. I veered left, right, and finally saw her. I kicked downward and reached out to grab her hand. I hooked an arm and pulled. Her face was all twisted and scary. She grabbed my arm with her other hand and jerked me toward her. I felt a *Whomp* in my stomach and doubled over, coughing out the last of my air. Pulling her to the surface I took in water.

Olivia and I coughed our way over to the ladder. My chest burned. Stomach cramped up. But I still had her by the arm. She looked pale. Brad and Sylvie leaned over the edge. "*What happened!?*"

Suddenly the lifeguard was there, helping us up the ladder. He sat us both down and hunched over Olivia.

Brad looked sheepish. "I was about to come...."

I coughed and stared him down. *So why didn't he?*

The lifeguard felt our pulses, checked us over, and after a few minutes he helped Olivia swim to shore.

Twig was waiting for us, fuming. "What happened?" Her shoulders heaving, Olivia looked down and kept quiet, so I answered.

"I thought she was in trouble, so I dove in looking for her."

Olivia's face was white. She folded her arms over her chest. Her saggy suit was twisted sideways, barely covering her.

"Olivia?" Twig asked gently. "What can you tell us?"

"I'm fine," she whispered, her head down. We all stood there.

"The raft is off limits to you all, for the rest of the day," the lifeguard barked. "And you," he said to me sternly. "Call for a lifeguard until you get your life saving certification."

Olivia turned away and I followed. "Are you really okay?" I asked her.

"Leave me alone," she grunted.

Wha-at?

I'm never saving anybody again.

Chapter Five

Brad, Sylvie and I lay on the sand for a few minutes. Before long the two of them were back in the water – Brad paddling around bragging about knowing everything cause his parents are forest rangers, and Sylvie laughing at him. I didn't feel like doing anything.

Twig was down the beach playing "Marco Polo" with the little kids. A few moms and dads were spread out on blankets while their toddlers dug in the sand.

I lay there, heart still pounding. Maybe stuffing my head into the sand could drive away this desperate feeling I had ever since I couldn't see Olivia under the water, when I thought she was drowning. What was she doing down there? Trying to *die*?

To sink into the deep, dark, water and never have to fight for anything again… never have to wake up … and look in the mirror … and hate what I saw….

Tears sneaked out from under my eyelids. I squeezed my eyes shut.

I won't think about this. Too scary. Olivia is just weird. Forget her. And something else I won't think about. The doll. What will I do about the doll?

The sand was a nest for me to hunker into. Warm. Soak up the sun. Ahhh …

"Todd Winslow?" It was Twig. "You planning to join us? Lunch time."

I must have fallen asleep. "I'm not hungry," I mumbled.

Twig squatted beside me. His green eyes flashed in the sunlight.

"Olivia's okay – right as roses. Come on, Winzo." He gave my arm a nudge. Then he stood up and walked back to the picnic tables under the trees.

When I closed my eyes again, I saw a doll sinking down underwater, her dress billowing up around her. Then Olivia floated down, her eyes looking dead. Then I came floating down behind her.

I shook it off and scrambled up from the sand. Hunted up my lunch and looked around for the others.

Brad and Sylvie saw me and waved me over to sit with them at a picnic table under the pine trees.

"Brad says he's had a MySpace for two years," Sylvie said to me. "Do you have one?"

"You have to be 14," I said. *And I don't need random people trying to meet me.*

Brad stretched, swelling his chest out. "If you're uncool, you get caught."

Just then Twig passed by with a sandwich and nodded.

"Sit with us, Twig!" Sylvie called out.

"Okay, just for a minute." He waved his floppy hat at the gnats as he climbed in to sit beside Brad.

"Winzo, the Bradman, and the girl from *Vogue* – happy as three clams at high tide," he said. Sylvie smiled. She liked him calling her the *Vogue* girl.

"Come on!" Brad groaned. "People in Maine really talk like that?"

"Ay–yuh, and then some...." Twig grinned at us.

"What's it like up there?" I asked.

"Finest kind of place," Twig said. The gold hairs on his arm glistened in the sun. "Maine's got the only two seasons a body needs – winter, and the Fourth of July."

Brad made a face like he'd heard that before.

"I spent pretty much my whole childhood with my Grandpa, way downeast in Machias."

Sylvie offered Twig a potato chip. "Down east? What's that supposed to mean?"

Twig grinned. "That means way up north. In Maine, the higher you go up the coast, the farther east you're heading. Say you're in Machias – If you get on a boat at the shore, and you sail due south – you'd hit Puerto Rico."

"Was your grandpa a lobsterman?" I asked him.

"No, my grandpa had a vegetable farm."

"What about your parents?" Sylvie mumbled, her mouth full of chips.

"My dad died when I was four, and my mom … well, she was sick for several years and couldn't take care of me."

"And your grandpa talked like that?" Sylvie asked.

"Ay – yuh, shouldn't wondah."

"Shoot him and put him out of his misery!" Brad groaned.

Sylvie looked down her nose. "Shut up, Brad,"

Twig gave him a poke. Brad poked him back.

"Did your grandpa give you the nickname Twig?" Sylvie asked.

"We're both named Thaddeus. My buddies called me Twig 'cause I was so thin back then."

"Is he still up there?" I asked.

"No, he passed on a few years ago."

"Here comes the old grandpa story!" Brad shook his head and gulped his soda.

Twig ignored him.

"Thaddeus was a real Yankee – gruff and silent and snug with his dollar. My teachers thought he was meaner than goose grease. He never came to my school, not to one basketball game or one parent conference. They didn't realize that he made me sit down every Sunday and tell him everything about my subjects."

Twig's lips scoot around loose like they're about to make a getaway.

"Grandpa would puff away on his pipe, hardly say a thing–just now and then, 'Have you told me all?' Then I'd pick up again and tell some more. 'Well, there you go,' he'd say if I'd done well – nod and puff away."

"If I got a low grade, he'd look me in the eye and smack his hand on the table. 'That ox won't plow. You hoist that one up, boy,' he'd say."

"Your grandfather never came to your basketball games?" Sylvie looked disgusted. "That's mean."

"Some of the other kids' folks hardly came either. I'd get extra attention from the teachers. They felt sorry for me, while all the time I knew my grandpa loved me." Twig chuckled.

"I think I'm gonna cry!" Brad teased. He pounded the table, sobbing.

Twig chuckled. "Ay – yuh. And I knew I needed to go to college, though he hardly ever said the word. But we'd go to the library every week and bring home books on every subject you could think of.

"I never had much spending money, but every week through the summer he'd put some of our earnings from the vegetable stand into a savings account for the university."

"And then you left him," Sylvie said. "And he was all alone."

"Waahh!" Brad sobbed some more. Twig grabbed Brad's head and held it under one elbow. Brad twisted up away.

"It was hard to leave him," Twig nodded. "But when he drove me up to Presque Isle, to the university – he grinned himself foolish the whole way. I'd never seen anything like it. Couldn't help himself – the old coot. He was still grinning and whistling when he hustled himself back into the truck and drove off. His face must'a been *some* sore later!"

"And we're getting *some* bored!" Brad complained.

"Shut up, Brad!" Sylvie waved him off.

"When I missed him," Twig went on, "I'd imagine him back home doing chores, laying the fire in the wood stove – and grinning when he thought of me studying, laying out a future for myself."

Twig left the person he loved most. But he knew his grandpa loved him. I don't know anymore about Dad. He never says he loves me. What if I had to leave Mom and Casey and Dad behind, for some reason? How could I survive?

"So!" Twig slapped his palms down on the picnic table and stood up. "Now you guys know why I keep the old lingo alive. I do it for him – keeps him by me."

"Easier to keep his picture in your wallet and give us a break!" Brad cracked.

Twig grinned and gave Brad a pat on the back as he left us.

"Twig's getting to be a real old faht," Brad said.

"Ay–yuh," I said. "And then some."

It's better to agree with Brad. Twig doesn't need me to stand up for him. Life will be so much worse if Brad starts in on me. I see him watching me out of the corner of his eye.

I'm careful how I move. I hold my shoulders stiff, so they won't swing, and I put my hands in my pockets a lot, so they won't wave around. But sometimes I forget.

*****

The next morning I was early and I went down to the Discovery room to visit Boxo the turtle. That obnoxious kid Foster was up on a stool, hunched over Boxo's tank.

"Hey, Foster, what are you doing?"

Foster whipped around and the screen banged on the tank.

"Nothin,' nothin.'" He was standing so I couldn't see into the tank.

I walked over closer.

"He's okay – he's fine." Foster held out his arms to stop me.

I faked to one side and leaned the other way to see.

"Foster! Jeez! You can't turn a turtle over on his back!"

Boxo was upside down. I saw his neck stretch all the way back and his head pressed into the wood chips. He arched his neck and tried to use his head to pivot his body back over.

"He's okay," Foster insisted. "He can turn over. I saw him do it."

I pushed Foster off the stool. "He's gonna smother." I reached in and turned him over. Boxo pulled his head and legs in and closed up his shell.

I wanted to punch the little monster.

"You want somebody to stick you in a garbage can headfirst and leave you there?"

"Awwww…"

"He could starve to death!" I yelled.

Foster stuck his chin out at me. "He's not gonna starve."

I lunged at him.

"Awww…." Foster turned and ran out the back door just as Twig came in the front.

"What's up with Foster?" Twig asked. I told him what happened.

Twig shook his head. "I'm about to tie that boy out on a rock for crow bait."

"Why don't you kick him out of camp?"

"Not yet. I'm hoping to show him how phenomenal animals are."

"I don't think he's getting it."

"Maybe not. But I'm not giving up, and the animals are safer if he's here in camp with us than they would be if he were out there loose on his own."

Twig soon had us at work building houses for bluebirds. I was sanding some pieces when Sylvie suddenly came up behind me and whispered in my ear.

"Time for my community service."

She strutted over to the next table where Olivia was working facing into the corner.

"Are you okay, Olivia? You looked upset at the lake yesterday, after...," she stammered, "you know...."

Olivia glanced up but didn't say a word. She looked back at her project.

Sylvie shifted from one foot to the other. "Well, anyway, I have an idea ... a project for you and me." She tilted her head and smiled down.

Olivia looked up with one eyebrow raised.

"It would be fun. I do makeovers for my friends, and I'm really good at it. We could do your nails, and pick a whole color scheme that works for you, and maybe a little makeup, and find a hair-style that goes with the shape of your face. You have nice eyes…"

It's true. Olivia does have nice eyes. And a pixie face. She could be pretty. She's a girl, so she's halfway there. Some people would pay everything they had even to be as plain as her. Why wouldn't she try to look better?

Sylvie talked faster, fluttering her hands around Olivia's head.

"…you know, like a whole professional makeover. Maybe we could go shopping together and get a nail kit, and makeup … and a good brush. It would be a gift from me to you." Sylvie clasped her hands together and smiled, eyes widening.

I held my breath.

Olivia looked Sylvie up and down – from the taupe eyeliner to her orange glitter flip-flops.

"Can you move?" Olivia said. "You're blocking the light."

Sylvie lurched back, her mouth dropping open. Then she spun around and stomped across the room and out the door.

I clamped a hand over my mouth.

Poor Sylvie! Her timing was lousy. Olivia was probably still upset about the underwater drama.

Olivia leaned back over her work, sanding furiously. Yeah, that's Olivia. And would there *ever* be a good time to try to change her?

I thought of Sylvie outside, fuming. I could go out and talk to her. Olivia looked over at me. Luckily, I wasn't smirking.

I tried to think of something to say to Olivia.

Wait a minute. Who got kicked in the stomach? That would be me. Why should I try to make it okay between them?

* * * * *

Twig's last project of the day was a scheme to teach us about shorebirds. Sylvie, Brad and I followed the path along the stream, looking for bird tracks in the mud. It was like a scavenger hunt, but instead of collecting things, we had clipboards where we'd check off the bird that made each set of tracks, and where we saw them. First Sylvie had to tell Brad the makeover story.

"I can't believe I missed it!" Brad grumbled. "Olivia dissing Sylvie!"

Sylvie turned on me with a sour smirk. "Saving her didn't do much for your girlfriend's personality."

"Cut it out. You know she's not my girlfriend. I don't even like her."

"You invited her out to the raft. You dragged her up from the bottom of the lake. And you heard me in there. I was 'Miss Congeniality' – wasn't I?"

"You tried, Sylvie."

She sighed, exasperated. "Okay, let's forget it. Let's look for tracks."

Why *did* she try the makeover? To impress Twig? Or maybe she *was* just trying to be nice.

We got busy looking over the drawings of birds' tracks on our papers. I never cared before what kind of foot a duck had, or a heron. But seeing the different marks in the mud and matching them up turned out to be cool.

Brad was leaning over a faint heron track we'd found. Three long toes.

"What if we find a track that's not on our list? A mystery bird, never seen before," I said.

"We should add an extra toe. That would really fake out the little shizbrats," Brad chuckled.

Sylvie held up four fingers stretched wide. "Oh, funny. Like 'Big Foot the Stalker Wading Bird.'"

She looked over at me. "Todd, you're too *nice* to do anything delinquent. Right?"

I didn't like her voice. "Go ahead. Do it," I told them. Brad grinned at Sylvie.

"But how?" Sylvie asked.

Brad broke a stick off a tree and held it out to Sylvie. "Draw it with this."

She hung back. "I don't want to get any muddier than I already am."

I gotta prove myself. I stepped up and jerked the stick out of his hand. "The shizbrats will go crazy trying to figure this out." I laughed, squatting down by the tracks.

I drew a faint outline of a long toe beside the three toes of the heron. It looked lame, but I kept at it until all the prints had an extra toe.

"Cool," Sylvie giggled. "But what if Twig sees *our* footprints?"

"We're supposed to be here. No big deal," Brad answered, leaning over me. "That'll do, Winzo."

As we wandered on, watching for trail markers, I was feeling good. The woods were green and ferny, and hidden birds were calling to each other – "EEE-cher, EEE-cher." Faker Todd might even survive.

We passed the pine with the jagged lightning gash down its trunk. I was in the lead, and I saw the next arrow nailed to a tree, pointing us to the right on a crossing trail. On a whim I sprang up to grab a branch overhead. I hung there for a second and dropped down. Of course Brad had to go one better. He jumped up to tap the wooden arrow fastened high on the tree. As he came down, the arrow rotated downward.

"Oops," Brad chuckled. We stood looking at it.

"The little kids will follow the arrow down into the Underworld," Sylvie giggled.

"Follow de wabbit, down the hole," I added, "like Alice."

"Now fix it," Sylvie told him.

Brad eyed the arrow. Then he thrashed around in the underbrush and came out with a long stick.

He poked at the arrow with his stick, swinging it up around slowly until it caught and stopped. It was pointing to the left.

I knew that was wrong. "No, we're supposed to go to the right. I saw it."

"You point like a girl, Winzo."

I froze.

"Brad!" Sylvie giggled. "Not nice."

Brad smirked. "Look, this is the way the arrow wants to point. Anyway, dem bawdy little fools could use some extra exercise. Come on let's go, before they get here."

Sylvie and I looked at each other. "Very amusing," she said. "They'd be so confused. But Brad. I think you have to change it back."

Brad grimaced. "Nah, why?"

I tried to think of a reason Brad might accept. "If we do more than one stunt, Twig's gonna freak, and zip goes all our freedom."

Brad's voice rose to a soprano, "There goes your voice uh-uh-up again, Wimpo. Just like Sylvie's."

"Cut it out, Brad," Sylvie said. "Todd's right. Twig will make us hold hands with the little kids."

"Yeah, okay, okay," Brad grumbled. "I'll fix it." He maneuvered the arrow around and around the nail until it pointed Right. He dropped the stick. "You go ahead and I'll catch up. I gotta take a pit stop."

I charged up the trail as fast as I could, back to the Center. How do the idiots always come up with 'Wimpo?'

After I checked in with the ranger in the office, Sylvie finally caught up. "Brad can be a total jerk. Don't let him get to you."

"No problem," I said.

When Brad finally showed up I kept my distance. I stayed over by the bulletin board to wait for Dad. Pinned up on the board was a newspaper story about a mixed-up crab. A waterman over in the Chesapeake Bay caught a crab that looked half male and half female. It had one blue claw and one red-tipped claw. He put it in a cage with a female crab to see what would happen. First the strange crab tried to mate with the female. Then it ate her, like competing females do.

Then I heard the ambulance siren.

Chapter Six

The ambulance should have taken *me* away. For the next 24 hours I got in trouble with just about everybody. But what happened first was – a ranger from the main office charged out the door and ran to meet the two medics as they stepped out of their ambulance. All three went trotting down the trail toward the stream.

Brad jumped up and hustled across the driveway. "Let's check out what happened!"

Good for you, Brad. You go on and get in the middle of it. Sylvie looked back at me as she straggled slowly over to the trail. "You coming?" she yelled.

"Nah, you tell me later," I answered.

Dad showed up a minute later. In the car I was thinking about the messed-up crab. I held up my hands and imagined one had blue nails and the other had red nails.

I looked out the window. *Huh?* Dad went the wrong way.

"Aren't we going to Casey's sitter's house?"

"No, I've got a surprise planned. Casey will stay later today."

We pulled up into a big parking lot. "Come on, get out."

Oh, great.

Dad opened the door of Fast Pitch America and nudged me in. "Awright. Let's whack some balls!"

Dad rented us a cage and handed me a helmet and a bat. In we went to the torture chamber. Like people in the Bible getting stoned to death. That's what it's like.

Dad turned the machine on and the first ball went whizzing by. I jumped back.

"Step into it quicker," he said.

"It's too fast."

"No, it's not. Come on – you can hit it if you try."

"Turn the speed down!"

"The speed is fine. Swing!" I swung and missed. The next one hit my knee. I went over to the side net for a second to rub my knee.

"Shake it off."

What's with Dad? I gritted my teeth to keep from swearing at him. *Is he still mad about the guy who came to the door? Or ... oh no ... did they find the doll??* I sank down to the mat. Balls were whacking against the back of the cage.

"You can't quit because you get a little bump, Todd. Listen, if *my* dad had ever taken me to fast pitch, I would've been psyched," Dad was saying. "I would've gone crazy."

If they found the doll – what would Dad do? Bring me to the batting cage to play boy games?

Dad glared at me. I looked away "Turn down the speed," I said finally. "I'm not getting up till you turn the speed down."

Dad went over and fiddled with the machine. The balls started coming slower. I got up – swung at a bunch – and missed. Then I hit one.

"You can do it," Dad forced a smile. "You've got good coordination. Remember all the times we went to the park to play T-ball and kick the soccer ball?"

"Oh yeah, I remember." *Better not ask me if I liked it, Dad.*

We took turns hitting. I could tip the balls pretty often – but when I finally got a solid hit, the force shook me right up my arms and rattled my teeth.

"See, this is great. You're getting it. Now let's try them faster."

Why doesn't he bring up the doll? If they found it, he would.

"Let me get used to this speed first."

"I could use more of a challenge," Dad grumbled. He was hitting most of them.

"So you hit and I'll watch," I said.

"Don't shy away from the ball."

"You want me to get hit in the head? These helmets are like cardboard."

I noticed two teenagers in the next cage looking over at us.

Dad grunted. "I took time off work today for *you.* I can't stand to see you always alone – rollerblading or whatever. That's no way to make friends. Like the coaches say – there's no 'I' in 'TEAM'. Brush up your skills, get on a team – then you'll have buddies. That sorry nature camp is over in a few days – then I want you to go to sports camp."

"Why not just pull me out right now?"

"Keep up this attitude and I *will.*"

"Shhhh!" I glared at Dad.

"You trying to hit me in the head?" the blond kid in the next cage squealed to his buddy, mocking me. He hugged his head girl-style.

"You scared, you wanna quit?" his ugly friend answered, grinning at us.

Dad gave a raw laugh, like he was on their side.

I took off my helmet and walked out the door, right out of Fast Pitch America.

When I get to the car, I'll find a magic silver bat on the back seat. *It's a present from Princess Aurora. I'll wait for those jokers behind the car. When they walk by – whack! Whack! I'll knock'em into space. They won't land crumpled in the parking lot. They'll orbit the earth a couple of times, screaming their heads off. Then they'll fall through the atmosphere and stick unhh! On the spines of a giant cactus – way out in Texas.*

Oh, yeah.

* * * * *

Mom and Dad didn't say a word about Prom Barbie. But after dinner that night I got a phone call.

"This is Olivia."

Gag. "You know my number?" I said.

"Twig gave it to me."

"He told you to call me?"

"Um … no."

I waited.

"Um …"

I wanted to yell at her. *Why are you so dopey?*

"It's about what happened at the lake." I could barely hear her.

"I guess you weren't trying to do anything," she went on. "Twig doesn't think you were…. I hate to be grabbed."

Huh?

"So you kicked me?"

"Especially by a boy."

"Oh. Thanks. You kicked me in the stomach. I was trying to *help* you."

"Well you grabbed me."

This is like talking to a robot toy. "I thought you were drowning and you kicked me, then you told me to stay away from you."

"Ummm… I apologize."

"You can swim, can't you?"

That irritated her. "I can *swim,*" she said.

"Well *sorry.* I mean if you're not that comfortable in the deep water, don't go out so far."

"I can swim. ItwasthewayIfell," she blurted. "My suit … got all twisted. I had to stay below and fix it."

"Oh." I remembered how weird the saggy suit looked, barely covering her, when we were on the beach. "Yeah, I get it."

I pictured her falling sideways and then her strap slipping off her shoulders. And trying to straighten that loose piece of rag, down under the water.

"The way you fell in. Did you slip?"

"I needed to get away."

"Really?"

"And I hate to be grabbed. I'm going."

Click.

She hung up.

* * * * *

The next morning Twig gathered us all together.

"Most of you know that one of our campers – Foster Berman – was hurt yesterday. He fell through the rotten boards on the abandoned trail down by the marsh. His leg is broken, so he won't be coming back to camp this session."

Foster, of course. It would be.

The younger kids oohed and nudged each other.

"Let's go over all the safety rules again, right now, starting with the importance of staying together and keeping to the marked trails. "

I turned to Brad and whispered," Did Twig notice the bird track we faked?"

"I don't know – who cares?"

"I'll tell him … in case…"

Brad leaned into my shoulder. "No, you won't. It's done. Who cares how it happened."

"Maybe Foster got confused and tried to follow the track we made, you know, to find the mystery bird or something. Went into the water, farther into the marsh and ended up getting hurt. Hey, did he say it was down by the streaked pine?"

"Shhhhh! Leave us out of it," Brad hissed. "You want us to get blamed for Foster screwing up his leg? "

"Maybe that arrow slipped down again and Foster didn't know which way to go."

"Zip it about the arrow!"

"Well, we changed it back the right way."

"Let it lie. Don't say a word about it, hear me?"

Brad squeezed my elbow, harder than he needed to.

"All right. All right."

Twig finished up his lecture and asked for volunteers to check the caterpillar chrysalis on the apple tree. I grabbed the chance to go outside. Brad can eat my dust.

We'd been checking the cocoon things every couple of days. I didn't get to see a caterpillar make one, but it's been cool anyway, seeing them changing. They start out kind of blue-green, and then start turning gray, getting darker and darker. The day I was absent the other kids saw a butterfly come out.

When I got to the apple tree I noticed Sylvie following me.

One chrysalis was clear now. Inside I could see tiny orange wings, all folded up.

Sylvie started talking about somebody she was mad at.

The chrysalis was shivering – not from the wind, but from the inside. Creepy. I looked closer. There was a rip at the lower end, where the head was – cause they hang upside down when they make their cocoon thing. Sylvie was still talking.

"...I can't believe he would leave me. He's always been crazy about me..."

"Some bug must have got in. Gross." I said. Sylvie was rambling on.

"…He taught me tennis and we played on weekends when I was…

The covering split right down the length of the chrysalis, and a black leg poked out. I jumped back and bumped Sylvie. The long leg waved around in the air.

"Ugh! What's that?" she whispered into my ear.

"Don't ask me. Hey – want to go get Twig?"

"He said we can watch if one is hatching."

The leg kept waving around like it was looking for something to grab onto. But the chrysalis was hanging apart from the branch like it's supposed to. If it's close to anything, even a blade of grass, the caterpillar will leave and look for another place where nothing will bump the chrysalis and make it deformed.

Sylvie kept talking about whoever.

The leg disappeared and another leg appeared on the other side. This leg grabbed the ripped edge of the chrysalis shell. Then another leg came out and held on. The thing started pulling itself out from inside the ripped chrysalis. The head came out first, then an ugly fat belly, like a slug, and then puny limp orange wings. That's a *butterfly*? Those wings couldn't carry an ant.

"…he doesn't treat me the same anymore. Since I got fat."

She was making no sense.

The creature lifted one of her long skinny legs and slowly stroked her back. An antenna came unstuck and waved in the air. I was inches away, afraid to breathe on it. Then the other antenna came loose, too, and waved all around. The sun was shining on her and she looked wet and glisteny, waving her antennae in all directions.

"She's talking about going back to the Hague… wherever that is."

I turned to her. "Sylvie, what are you talking about?"

"The Netherlands! There is absolutely nothing in the Netherlands! Who's even heard of it? Can you imagine *me* there?"

"Why would you go there and who says you're fat?"

"Not me… my mother. You're not even listening!"

"What did you say?"

"Mom keeps trying to tell me stuff – about their marriage. I don't want to hear it! She'll say, 'he just doesn't respect me, ever since I got fat.' She *is* fat. But so is he! Why are they ruining my life?"

The butterfly was changing! Her wings weren't so limp. And maybe her stomach was getting smaller. I saw a shiny ant crawl up next to her and touch her with his antennae. Ants can't eat a butterfly, can they? The ant went back the way it came.

"Omigosh," Sylvie kept on, "I'll end up with my mother and she'll be depressed and crying all the time!"

I met Sylvie's mother a couple of times. I'm surprised she can hold her neck up with all those heavy gold necklaces. It's true she's chubby, but I like her accent. I think she shouldn't wear such tight skirts. They make her look bigger. I only saw her Dad once – he was big, too, but I didn't notice anything special about him.

"What if your parents said they were getting a divorce – what would you do?" Her voice got all soft and croaky.

I got enough problems already.

This should distract her. "Hey, look – she's…it's pumping up its wings. See, they're getting bigger!"

"…and my father travels all the time. How could I live with him? Live in some hotel? No. They have to quit it and make up."

Something like a stick came out of the butterfly's head. *What's that?* It disappeared again, rolled up like a tiny spring, up to where a mouth should be.

"We're *happy*," she insisted. "He's happy, she's happy, I'm happy. They're *not* getting divorced. I'm *not* putting up with a stepfather, or a stepmother. Or a *stepsister* for heaven's sake."

"That's gotta be the tongue," I said. "Sylvie, look how she can roll up her tongue and unroll it. That's how she must get the sugar stuff out of the flowers."

It was incredible. She really looked like a butterfly now. Her wings were drying and she moved them very slowly back and forth. They were orangey-yellow, and sparkled in the sun. The wings were so much bigger now. All the juice from that fat belly pumped into her wings so they unwrinkled and spread out.

"See all the ants?" Sylvie finally noticed something. A line of ants was rushing over the branch, headed for the butterfly.

I tried to brush them off the branch. They might kill her before she even lives one day. I know they have jaws.

"Ooh, they're on me!" Sylvie was in my way, hopping and jiggling and flinging her arms around.

"Move!" I said. They were on me, too, and hard to brush off. I hated touching them. Their bodies were like shiny armor. A whole long army was coming. I looked back at the butterfly.

Two big ants climbed on her.

The butterfly poked them with her antenna. All of a sudden she flapped her wings and lifted off. I saw one ant fall through the air. The butterfly flapped a few times and was way up over our heads. I couldn't tell if she was okay. The flight was jerky. I hope the ant's not biting her. I hope her wings were ready. Fly away butterfly. Before someone steals your life.

"You're not even listening. Todd!"

"I know lots of kids with divorced parents," I said, watching the butterfly flutter down again in little bounces. I ran over as she lit on the butterfly bush. She was okay. The ant was gone. She crawled up onto the flowers and poked her mouthstick into the openings, one after the other. She's great. She's beautiful.

I looked at Sylvie. Her eyes were red and glaring at me. "You care more about that stupid bug," she said, and walked away from me.

Chapter Seven

That was Number Two in Todd's Series of Unfortunate Events. Both Sylvie and Brad turned their backs on me for the rest of the day.

I couldn't wait to get away. After camp Dad dropped me at Casey's sitter's house and told me to walk her home. Casey saw me and went inside to collect her stuff. I stayed out in the yard. Her annoying little freckled friend Amanda was digging in the flowerbed with a trowel and staring at me.

"Keep staring like that, and your eyes are gonna fall out," I warned her. She gave me a look.

"You play with dolls," she said.

I choked. "No way."

"Casey says you do."

"Well I don't. She's crazy."

Amanda was pulling on each end of a worm and watching me. I turned and walked down to the sidewalk. Whatever she was going to do to the worm, I didn't want to see it. Under my shirt sweat tickled my chest.

Casey came out with her backpack and we started home.

"You told that little freak that I play with dolls? Are you crazy?!"

Casey frowned up at me.

"You do play dolls with me."

"I'm only doing that for you! To keep you company!"

Casey pouted. "Amanda's in second grade. She says boys aren't supposed to play with dolls. Especially big boys."

"Boys *don't* play with dolls. Do you see me with a bunch of dolls in my room?"Casey hung her head and held her hands over her ears. Her light hair hid her face like a silky fringe.

I got prickles on the back of my neck. *If anybody hears about this….*

"Don't tell her anything about me! And don't ever say that! Especially *that*!" I unlocked the front door and Casey started up the stairs. "You think I'm ever going to play with you again?"

"I'nnot playing with *YOU!*" she yelled. We scurried to our rooms and slammed our doors.

Thanks for blabbing, Casey. Now even the seven-year-olds think I'm weird.

I grabbed the fairy tale book and hurled it into the closet. It smashed against the wall. I fell back onto the bed.

What a pile of grief I've gotten about dolls. My whole life. When I first went to school, kids teased me when I said I liked Barbies. Even some of the girls were mean about it. So finally I gave up and pretended I didn't like them. Then Casey was born and dolls were finally allowed in the house. Mom and Dad got weird when I wanted to play with them. So when a boy came over to visit, we might steal one of her dolls and parachute it out the window or stick it up high in a tree. We even burnt one up in a bonfire. Dad thought *that* was pretty normal. But Casey couldn't understand why I'd play so nice with her, then turn into a monster when another boy came over. I had to do it to prove I was a boy.

I took Prom Barbie out of the clarinet case and hid her inside the back of my computer monitor. She's bent and scrunched up inside the hard plastic.

"You stay where you are," I whispered. "You're safer in there."

* * * * *

The next morning at camp Sylvie and Brad were still ignoring me. Probably laughing at me. I felt lame. Why did I shut out the one person who's actually nice to me at camp? Yesterday Sylvie was trying to tell me about her parents and I didn't listen. Now I'll have nobody to talk to.

We were supposed to finish nailing together our bluebird houses. I had just sat down alone at a table when I saw Olivia heading in my direction.

Oh, no.

I got up. "Excuse me," I said, squeezing past her. She and I ain't gonna start a Misfits Club.

Nothing ventured, nothing gained, like they say. I edged over toward Brad and Sylvie's table. Sylvie looked like a butterfly, dressed in a black and orange striped top and black shorts. I broke into their conversation.

"Olivia has some serious weirdness going on. And she says *boys* are aliens."

Sylvie's eyebrows perked up. "What did she say? Are you making it up?"

"I'm not making it up. It's true. She doesn't trust boys. That's what she told me."

Sylvie was hooked. "Really? When was this?"

"She called me a couple of nights ago."

"She called you? I told you she had a thing for you!"

"No… she was supposedly apologizing. She's scary."

Brad shot me the lifted eyebrow. "She's not the only one. But go on, what did she say?"

I glanced around. Olivia was only a couple of tables away. "'Boys are evil. You can't trust them.' That's what she said. Then she hung up on me."

"She may be on to something," Sylvie smirked.

"That's why she kicked me while we were underwater, I guess. While I was trying to save her."

Sylvie pursed her lips. "I didn't know she kicked you."

"Oh, yeah, right in the ... balls."

"Unh, hunh. No wonder you've been talking funny – way up there," Brad waved his hand up high as his voice rose to a squeak.

"I'm feeling a little strange," I groaned, as low as my voice could go. "Do you think she's put a curse on me?"

Sylvie squeezed my arm. "Yes, she did. That's why you've been such a dick and completely ignored me yesterday."

Brad frowned down at the squeeze. "I heard that something pretty weird happened in her family awhile ago ... don't remember exactly ...." Then he grinned. "Olivia's like a fart. Comes out of nowhere to stink up your life. And then ... evaporates."

Sylvie burst out laughing. "Todd, stick with us so she doesn't get her fungal fingernails into you."

Brad did not look pleased.

* * * * *

Later I saw Olivia alone looking at the butterflies. This time it's her or me. Take no prisoners. She doesn't need me anyway. She doesn't need anybody. She's totally lost in every project, huddled over the microscope with some bit of moss or a dead bug she found. Or her long thin fingers are probing a pine cone, like the butterfly's tongue invading a flower.

She's a planet of her own, an uninhabited planet.

Chapter Eight

Unhhh ... somebody's shaking me ... I'm so tired ....

"Hey, buddy–you overslept .... Time to get up!"

Unhhh ... it's Dad ... I wanna sleep ....

"Come on, kid. Monday morning ... you gotta get up ... covers off! Whoa ... what's this you're wearing?

"What's this you've got on? Todd! Wake up ... what the ...?? Wake up!!"

"Hunhh?"

"What are you doing with a *DRESS* on???"

Oh no ... Oh no. "Un ...Unh ...."

"You look like a ..." Dad rushed out to the hall "MARY!!!" he bellowed. "MARY!! Come up here!"

I jumped out of bed, staggered across to Casey's room, pulled off the skirt and stuffed it into her drawer. She was sitting up in bed, looking scared.

"Toddie?"

I ran back to my room, pulled on shorts and a shirt, and was sitting on the bed when my parents came in.

"Where is it?? Where's the dress?!" Dad demanded.

"In Casey's drawer."

"Go get it!!"

I got up and walked back into her room. She still sat frozen, looking scared. I pulled open the drawer and brought out the skirt.

"Why is Daddy ....?" She whispered. I headed back into my room. I handed him the skirt. He held it up.

"Can you explain to me why MY SON is wearing this thing to bed??"

"Casey and I were just..."

"Louder! I can't hear you!"

I looked at the floor and lied. "We were just playing a game – I forgot to take it off. I just fell aslee..."

"A game? A GAME of dress-up?? Dress-up is NOT a 13-year-old boy GAME!!!"

"That's my old skirt," Mom gasped. "I thought I gave that away .... Todd, I can't believe you are *still* dressing up!"

"Casey!! Get in here!" Dad yelled.

Casey came in, clutching her baby blanket. I shouldn't have said...

"You and Todd were playing dress-up last night?" Dad rumbled.

'No, we weren't', she's going to say....

"Uh-hunh."

"Yes??"

"Yeah," she whispered.

"You are never, EVER, TO PLAY DRESS-UP with Todd again. DO YOU UNDERSTAND??"

"Okay, Daddy." She started blubbering. "S-s-sorry."

I clenched my muscles to keep from bursting out crying.

"It's not her fault, Darren." Mom said.

"I'm going to make sure this NEVER happens again!!" Dad yelled.

Casey crumpled to the floor.

"And you!" He turned back to me. "What the... What is wrong with you?! Grow up! You want people to think you're a ..."

"Todd, you're way, way too old to dress up like this," Mom groaned.

"Why didn't you get rid of all the dress-up stuff in the whole house?" Dad yelled at Mom.

"Well... Casey...." Mom stuttered.

"I've told him," Dad said. "He has to shape up! For *years* I've been telling him!

"Come on, get tough. Spar with me!" Dad jerked me up off the bed. I held my palms up, trying to calm him down.

Slap … Slap… . He started slapping my palms.

"Let's go! Come on! Spar like a man!"

"Darren – what's the point of …"

"Daddy!" Casey wailed. Dad's face twisted, furious – like he was protecting the family from a monster.

"Come on! Fight back! Fight back!!"

I pushed against his hands. He grabbed my fingers and pushed back and forth, then sideways. I was falling ….

The back of my leg hit the edge of the bed and my knee buckled. I fell back, and my other leg kicked up fast.

"Aggghh!" Dad yelled, doubled over.

He gurgled, "Bastard!" groaning and holding his balls.

Mom and Casey's mouths hung open.

What's he going to do to me when he gets up??

Dad was swearing and moaning.

"Darren, he didn't mean to kick you – did you Todd?" Mom asked. Dad squinted up at me, then rolled over onto his side on the floor, groaning and slowly stretching out his legs, one at a time. I kept quiet.

"Todd! Apologize to your father!"

I opened my mouth, but nothing came out. Something had ahold of my throat.

The doorbell rang. Mom looked at me. We were frozen. It rang again. I looked over at my clock. 8:00. Nothing made sense.

Dad was breathing loud and slow, trying to catch his breath

"It's Mrs. Simmons!" Mom whispered, horrified. "She's giving you a ride today!"

Nature camp. I looked around the room for my shoes. *Get out of here*! I saw some beach thongs in the corner. I grabbed them and squeezed past Dad. He threw out one arm, to grab my leg. I jumped over it and ran. Down the stairs ...flung open the front door. No lunch. My heart was pounding. No backpack. Just get away.

* * * * *

Camp.

I couldn't even talk, I was so burned. Good thing I wasn't paired with Brad. Twig teamed me up with Olivia. Then he sent us out with paper bags to collect stuff off the ground to make nature mobiles.

What was Dad doing in my room, anyway? He should mind his own business – don't be pulling off my covers! What if I was naked? Stupid sparring – I wasn't even awake. Keep his hands off me. I got him back, didn't I? I didn't mean to, but I got him back good. Right in the balls. He was down there rolling on the floor. Maybe he's still there. Or maybe he had to go to the hospital.

Olivia scurried ahead of me collecting like crazy, pouncing on scraps – like Boxo pouncing on a worm. She kept wandering deeper into the woods.

I didn't care if we got lost – if we never came back.

What's Dad going to do to me? I don't want camp to be over. Let it just go on and on. Maybe I'll hide out here in the woods for a while. I could swipe stuff from the center and survive. The whole rescue squad would be out looking for me. Dad would think I was dead. Then he'd be sorry.

I'd go to a secret grove in the woods. Princess Aurora will come floating down through the trees. She'll wrap a green cape around me, and I'll be invisible. We'll fly off and Dad and the rescue guys, all covered with dirt and leaves, will see this green shape floating away, just out of reach. Yeah.

Yeah.

* * * * *

We heard the four whistles and headed back. When we got inside, Sylvie waved me to come over, but Twig frowned and pointed at Olivia. So I followed Olivia. Whatever. I won't be talking to anybody. Olivia ignored me, her head bent over her loot, sorting it with her thin fingers.

I tossed down the bark and acorns and pinecones I'd grabbed at the last minute. My stuff was trash, and I could care less. Twig passed around a box of driftwood for the top piece, some string to hang from it, and a box with feathers and snail shells. I took a couple of pieces of wood and some feathers without even looking at them.

Why did I have to fall asleep in that skirt? I could've just stuck it back into my closet, into that giveaway bag. Maybe I *did* take it off. I remembered the soft satin sliding down my leg. And I stepped out of it, and opened the closet door ...

Loser, you didn't take it off. You wore it. He found it. You don't have a dad any more.

Tears oozed out of my eyes.

I looked at the chunks of wood I was squeezing into my palm. One piece looked like a girl standing with her legs together. I fiddled with the feathers. Two gray feathers, one on each side – could make a fairy, or an angel. If I had more wood pieces like this one, and more feathers, I could hang two or three from the crosspiece. The fairies would hang down at different lengths from strings. Get some moss or something to glue on for hair.

Wrong. I would never dare. Not here. Not anywhere.

What's Dad going to do to me? It's going to be something big. Probably throw me out of the house. Where could I go? Would Grandma take me in? Grandma, who gets a headache every time noisy kids visit?

It was just a stupid skirt. It's not like I do drugs, or kill people. But hey, I'm a criminal.

I bent the girl piece till it broke.

"Where's your mobile, Winzo?" Twig was beside us.

"Didn't make one," I said, looking away.

"You okay man?" Twig put his hand on my shoulder.

I shrugged it off. Get off me or I'll cry!

"I'll be fine," I said.

Twig turned to Olivia. "Wow. Finest kind, Liv," he said softly.

After a few minutes I looked over. Olivia had glued a bunch of stuff to a long piece of bark. It wasn't even a mobile. It didn't have any string on it at all.

Her big owl eyes looked at me from behind dusty glasses.

I leaned over a little closer.

It was a dark wavy shape made of acorns, little bits of dark bark, berries, and dark gravel. And she'd used white round gravel to make dots all over. Near one end, there were two raised bumps.

I stared at it, and all of a sudden I saw it, like those hidden pictures that you have to look at cross-eyed before you see the shapes.

"It's a salamander...," I said.

She nodded, touching it gently with her thin fingers, pushing the gravel down into the glue. "Plannin' on fortunes," she said softly.

"What?"

"*Pleth-o-don four-chen-sis.*"

"Oh."

Wow ...she knows the scientific name. Her spotted salamander was like something you see in a museum. Like designs made of tiny tiles from the rich Roman people's houses. How did she do it?

All the kids were putting their mobiles on the shelf to dry. Across the room Brad and Sylvie were laughing together at something.

I scooted away from Olivia.

I'd been avoiding Brad, because I couldn't pull off an act. But after camp he came over to me. I didn't want to answer any questions, so to distract him I described Olivia's salamander.

"Really?" he said, looking doubtful. "I guess she's one of those retarded kids who can only do one thing – and she does salamanders."

Then Sylvie joined us.

"You've been weird today," she said to me. "Are you in trouble at home?"

Whoa, this girl has animal instincts! "Why do you think that?" I asked.

"Did you get busted?" Brad was very interested. "Go, Todd! What did you do?"

I tried to think of something to say.

We heard a horn beep and Brad looked over at the parking lot . "I gotta go. Tell me tomorrow!" He ran off.

Sylvie raised one eyebrow. "Come on, Todd … you can tell me."

"It's no big deal, Vogue."

"Did your little sister get you in trouble?"

Omigosh. CASEY. I hadn't thought of her all day. She lied for me. Why did she lie for me? I got her into it …. I told my parents we were both playing make-believe …. But who cares? Casey's not really in trouble. A girl isn't going to get into trouble playing dress-up. I'm the one who's toast. Worse than toast. I'm gonna be annihilated.

"Well?" she demanded.

"My dad's being a jerk. Like yours."

Sylvie looked more sympathetic. She patted my arm. "It sucks, doesn't it? I've been telling my dad straight up how awful it would be if he leaves us. He just looks at me with his helpless fish-face. I don't know what's going to happen. At least he's listening."

I'll never be able to tell Dad how I feel. It'd be easier if he left.

* * * * *

All evening I stayed in my room. I dreaded seeing him. Mom kept Casey busy chatting, pretending everything was normal, but Dad didn't even come home for dinner. He called and said he was working late.

Finally she came into my room, frowning and pinching her lips together. "You and I and your father have to talk about this sometime." She looked around the room like the right words might be hanging on the wall somewhere.

"You know, Todd, there are plenty of girls who think you are very good-looking. And nice. Remember the girl who was calling you last spring? And now this Olivia ... is she someone you're interested in?"

That's just sad. I glanced up at her, then went back to my video strategy guide. I knew what she was saying. *You're not supposed to like dresses. You're supposed to want to go out with girls.* I get a sick feeling every time this romance thing comes up.

"You've always been a wonderful son," she said. "You were so good with Casey when she was a baby. I loved being with the two of you. There was never any bickering. You were happy when you were helping me. So considerate. You never gave us any trouble...."

So they liked me when I was little. What about now? "Try telling that to Dad," I said.

She sighed.

"He's very upset. He is trying. Being a father is very important to him. You know *his* father was never very reliable. Your Grandpa was off losing money at the racetrack when he should have been home with his family."

I don't see what my *grandfather* has to do with anything.

Later, just as I was heading to bed, Dad came down the hall. I guess I'm invisible. He brushed past me and didn't even speak.

I went to my room, opened the monitor case, and pulled out Prom Queen Barbie. I looked into her sapphire blue eyes.

"They don't want me the way I am," I told her.

Chapter Nine

I had a lousy dream. I was wandering around in some big city and couldn't find my way. A friendly-looking guy was leaning against a fence and I asked him for help, but he tried to steal my backpack. When he started chasing me, I woke up.

Lying in my bed, I could hear faint voices. Must be my parents talking. I got up and tiptoed to the door. It was Dad.

"You knew this was going on? You knew he was dressing up like a girl?"

"Darren! That is so ridiculous. Come on!"

"You must have seen something."

"As far as I know, he hasn't done it for years." Mom answered.

"He still *is* – he's hiding it. What else are we going to find in his room?"

I leaned against the door frame, trying not to make any sound.

Dad went on. "Good thing he ran off that morning. I just about lost it."

"Darren, don't you dare."

"Well, did I touch him?"

Somebody groaned. "I just can't believe it. I thought he outgrew that … phase," Mom said.

"He's never been super-masculine," Dad said.

"But what's wrong…what's going on with him?"

"I wouldn't know. I never wanted to be a girl. Never wanted to wear pantyhose."

I hate the way they talk about me! But I couldn't move.

"He won't have any friends if he acts – girly – at school," Mom said.

"Who has he been spending time with?"

"He's always gotten along with girls, but he hasn't been close to a boy for awhile. I don't know what happens to them," Mom said.

"Why does he have to be weird? My one and only son."

"I know, Darren."

"I thought we'd be buddies. Try all the sports. Forget that. He's got the build. He's coordinated. He can run; he's got endurance. But he just refuses …. Why would he drop off the soccer team?"

"He *was* on the soccer team when we used to find Casey's lacy socks in his room. Oh, Darren …

remember … was he eight? When he told you he was half girl and half boy?"

"How could I forget?"

My chest squeezed tight. No air to breathe.

"And I told him he was all boy," Dad went on, "One hundred percent, and to stop watching those foolish animé cartoons – the big-eyed little girls with the baby voices. You probably let him keep on watching that stuff!"

"Stop it. You think it's my fault, don't you," Mom said. "You think I raised him to be this way."

I hung on to the door frame, gasping for a breath. *What if they hear me?*

"Well where did he get the skirt?"

"It was in a bag to donate! Maybe it was just this one time – playing dress-up. Maybe playing with Casey reminded him.... Darren, sometimes I think we were wrong. That we shouldn't have made a big deal about him wanting a doll when he was little … or stopped him from putting towels on his head to make long hair. Maybe we shouldn't have been so harsh. He could have tried on my dresses …"

"What? Encourage him? That would have made it worse!"

"But forbidden fruit – always tastes sweeter. He never got to try them, so he couldn't forget …"

"And where would it stop? When he wore a dress to first grade? No, we had to nip it in the bud."

"Or maybe – when he got to play the way he wanted for a little while – it would just ...evaporate. He wouldn't need it anymore."

"Don't be naïve. What decent parent would take that risk?"

I hugged my arms to keep from shivering.

"You sound ... terrible," Mom said.

"This *is* terrible."

"Maybe he doesn't want to grow up. To be a man."

"Like me. Thanks a lot."

"Oh, *Darren.* I don't know. But you can stop blaming me." Her voice went way high.

Somebody sighed. There was more mumbling. I heard tight sobs. Mom was crying.

I crept across to my bed and lay in the dark, shaking.

They were blaming each other for their freak son. It hurt so much. And there was nobody I could tell. Nobody.

The way they talked about me was so mean. Like they were talking about dirt.

They'll never forget the dumb things I did when I was little.

I suddenly remembered the magic show we went to when I was about six. I was so pumped. In the middle the magician asked the audience to name our favorite trick and I yelled out, "Can you turn me into a girl??" All the people around us gasped. My parents looked like they'd swallowed chalk.

I was only *six.*

Now my stomach twisted in knots.

What am I going to do?

* * * * *

I didn't want to go to camp. I wanted to stay in bed forever. But I couldn't face Dad. So I went. But how will I fake it for Brad? He'll hate me even more if he finds out what Dad found out. Everybody will.

I went in to visit Boxo. Lifted him out of the tank and looked at him. His eyes glowed brown, yellow, and green like a church window.

Princess Aurora could change him into a flippered sea turtle, and a tiny mermaid could ride on his back. A whole army of turtles, swimming with mermaids on their backs. No, I'd be in the lead, on Boxo, challenging all the evil powers of the deep. With our magic tridents we'd turn the bad sharks into sea snails.

Dad's twisted angry face floated up in front of me. All the mermaids and the turtles disappeared.

Come back! Help me!

I'm not saving anybody. I'm such a joke. Stupid make-believe. Dumb-ass box turtle. Moron. I can be a bastard too. Just watch me.

Smash Boxo on the wall! Break him wide open! Pull out his guts!

NO!

I clutched Boxo to my chest. Tears rolled down my face.

"I almost hurt you, stupid. Get away from me."

* * * * *

All morning, I was wondering…where do I hide Barbie? When can I get out to the woods? Because Barbie was in my backpack right under the table. Last night I couldn't sleep… thinking – they're gonna search my room. I know they are! I never meant to keep Barbie for this long, anyway. I could put her in Casey's room – mixed in with her other dolls. Mom and Dad wouldn't notice one more. But Casey would notice. I could say … I found it? Tell her I bought it for her? Beg her not to tell?

NO … I couldn't expect her to lie for me again. I'll have to throw her away, or I'll get caught with her.

I knew they'd be coming in – snooping, digging through all my stuff, with no search warrant. I'm – a suspect. No, I'm a criminal.

I got up and pried Barbie out of the monitor case. I put her in my backpack, wrapped up in my rain jacket. Mom never looks in my backpack. It was the only way to get her out of the house, *today.*

After we watched the movie about orienteering, Twig called me aside. "Winzo, we're going to practice compass orienteering and I'm teaming you up with Olivia. Don't let her get lost, okay?"

I rolled my eyes and groaned. Twig squeezed my shoulder. "Thanks, Buddy."

Olivia wandered over to me, wearing binoculars on a strap around her neck.

Twig handed out a compass to each team. It was a rectangle with a round compass inside. Inside the compass circle the arrow bobbled around. Half of the arrow was black and half was red. The rest of the rectangle was clear plastic and had 3 parallel red lines.

"Okay, guys," Twig said. "The red and black arrow is called the compass needle. The red end will always point toward the North Pole, the earth's magnetic north. Unless you're carrying a pocketful of iron. That might confuse the compass. Is anyone carrying iron?" We checked our pockets and took out anything metal.

"The circle around the compass is called the housing. Turn it, you'll see that it rotates." Olivia and I hunched over the compass. It did turn. But the red arrow inside didn't move. Cool.

"The straight line on the plastic case is the travel arrow." Twig showed us how to pick a direction we wanted to go and turn the housing so that direction, like Southwest, pointed toward the big travel arrow. Then we turned our whole bodies, keeping our compass flat in our hand, until the compass needle pointed North again. Then we knew which way to start walking, following the travel arrow. Very cool.

"You won't get too lost, because there are roads within a mile of us in each direction. Muncaster is southeast, and Norwood is northwest. But nobody should be going anywhere near that far."

I put on my backpack when our teams went outside to test direction-finding. Then Twig gave us maps showing the targets each team needed to find, and sent us off.

It was strange being with Olivia. We didn't talk, and I was glad. When she had the compass, she just plotted the course and walked off. I plodded along behind her. Suddenly she'd stop and lift her binoculars to scan the woods and find a bird. She and I are so different. I never forget anybody who's behind me. If I forget, I might do something stupid. Olivia is strange …but smart. I couldn't believe how fast she got us to the target, even with all the distractions. But I did notice her looking at me a few times – more than usual.

I didn't talk, either, when it was my turn to set our course. I messed up a few times. Once I had the black end of the needle aligned with North instead of the red end. So we were going the opposite direction, and had to go all the way back to the last target and plot over again. Olivia didn't say a word as I swore and fumed. She had found a caterpillar.

We had just reached the last target, a bright green ribbon tied to a tree with our team number on it, when we heard the whistle, signaling that our time was up. Through the trees I could see the other teams straggling back to the Center.

This is it. Has to be.

"Go ahead Olivia, I'll be there in a couple of minutes."

Olivia looked at me for a second and nodded. You never had to explain to Olivia. She turned away. I backed behind a bush and shoved the compass into my pocket.

I wandered a few steps up the trail and looked back. Didn't see her. I hustled off-trail into the brush, looking for a hidden place. I had about five minutes to say goodbye to Barbie before someone came looking for me.

I crashed through the sharp branches, thorns ripping at my arms. In a little clearing was a spruce tree with branches right to the ground. I dug at the soft soil with my heel. Then I grabbed a pointed rock and pierced the soil, pulling tufts out with my fingers until I'd made a hole.

I sat down and took Barbie out of my pack. I smoothed the shiny material of her blue dress, touched the tiny bumpy necklace, and stroked her hair.

Bury her? Stick her in the ground – with the dirt all over the blue silk? It was like *murder.*

"I'm sorry. I don't know what else to do."

The branches above were swaying gently, kindly. I'm not burying her in the dirt. I tucked her into my pack again, put it on, and wiggled through the dense branches to the prickly trunk. There were plenty of big branches for footholds, but the trunk was a porcupine's back, scratching my face and arms and tugging at my pack with every step. I made it up 10 feet and clung to a branch, unlooped my pack, and took Barbie out.

"I'm not sticking you in the dirt. At least you can be out in the air." I reached as high as I could and sat her in a tuft of needles. "Please be okay," I whispered. Barbie smiled up at the sky. "Maybe someone will find you and you'll have a home."

Home. Mom. Casey.

Casey knew why Dad was upset. She's no innocent baby anymore. Bug-eyed Amanda made sure of that. Every day Casey asked me – "Todd, you can't play dolls with me now – right? You can't read the Little Mermaid to me – right? Can you read another story to me? Can you still come in my room?" I finally told her I didn't know the answers to half the questions and please stop asking.

I guess Little M will always be stuck in the story where we left her last time we played – trying to get the Prince to fall in love with her. She's frozen, with her mouth open, wanting to tell the

Prince who she really is. *They're in the palace and she's leaning toward him. He's looking confused. This mute girl is trying to communicate. Through the big stone window of the castle you can see fields where peasants are working. Sun is shining on Little M's face. Her pleading eyes say, "Love me, love me, even when you find out who I really am..."*

I struggled down the trunk.

Barbie will be all alone. In the dark and the rain, with crows coming to peck at her shiny eyes. Stupid. My fault. I should have left her in the store.

Goodbye, Barbie.

Why do Mom and Dad remember every stupid thing I said when I was little? I know I'm a boy. I never tried to cut off any body parts! I just ... I like what I like. Why is it a crime?

They'll never forget. They'll never forget that I had a skirt on, once, when I was 13. I might forget about it, but they never will.

If Barbie has to go, I have to go too. Leave everything behind. So they won't have to live with their defective son. Never have to look at him again.

I pulled the compass out of my pocket. What did Twig say? Norwood Road is northeast? That'll take me to Rt. 95. I'll hitchhike. Go south. Or go north. I can work for food.

I held the compass flat and plotted northeast, toward Baltimore. Checked the red point. Yep, GO.

Chapter Ten

I sighted on the thickest tree I could see in the northeast and headed for it, crashing through the brush. So many trees the same size! Which one did I aim for? I had to stop and pull out the compass again. Pick something that stands out, Twig said. One tall tree was leaning … there's my target. Pricker vines were everywhere, snagging my arms and bare legs. I had to detour around thick bushes of thorns, but I was scared of getting off track. When I finally got to the leaning tree, I checked the compass again and sighted on a big rock across a stream. Down the slope I skidded, leaped the creek and slipped, fell on a rock, got up and slogged up the bank. Sighted again, and jogged through a stand of pines. With every thud I heard Little M's sisters calling, "Make *haste*, make *haste*, either you or he must *die*!" like drumbeats in my head.

I busted through forests of ferns and monster vines strangling the trees, over dead fallen logs and poison ivy. Almost from under my feet, birds burst up screeching and took off, beating their wings frantically.

Was that the sound of traffic? Checked the travel arrow. Huh? North? I'm off course. But that must be a road. My ride out of here. I turned toward the sound and ran faster. Saw cars passing through the trees. I staggered out onto the shoulder of a two-lane road. Ran to the black-top and stuck out my thumb. The fifth car pulled over, a white van.

"Don't get into that truck!" a voice screamed. I looked back. Olivia stepped out of the trees.

"What are you doing here, you freak?" I yelled. "Leave me alone!"

She looked frantic – eyes bugged out and her mouth drawn back. "If you get into that truck ... I ... I'll tell ... I'll tell everybody about the doll you put in the tree."

My stomach flipped. I could see Dad looking up into the tree, shaking his head in disgust.

"So what? I won't be here. I'm never coming back." The truck drove off. "See what you did? Get out of here!"

I stuck out my thumb again as two cars zoomed by. Olivia squatted down on the side of the road, panting.

I edged away from her, further along the road. "Who else is with you?"

Olivia jumped up and followed. "Nobody."

"Why did you follow me?"

"I just did."

A car full of teenaged guys stopped. The back door opened. I went over.

"Don't do it!" Olivia called, running up behind me.

I leaned my head into the back seat. A face full of metal piercings leered at me. I put one foot in.

"No!" Olivia screamed, shaking the open door.

The sketchy guy in back reached for my arm. "Make up your mind, kid." A creepy feeling hit me and I wavered. Olivia jerked the neck of my tee shirt and dragged me backward. I sprawled onto the gravel.

I heard "Whathefu…!" The door slammed shut, the engine roared, and gravel buckshot sprayed my legs.

"Leave me alone!" I screamed. "You crazy … dork whacko! Why are you haunting me?"

Olivia hunched over me. "If you go, I go."

"That's totally insane!" I rubbed the snot off my face, rolled onto my knees and started to stand. She dropped down, grabbed me by the ankle and pulled me down again. I tried to jerk my leg away.

"You think you're a loser, but you're not," she gurgled, her face wrinkled up, eyes wild. I could barely understand her "You think there's nobody else like you, nobody as screwed up as you."

"You're more screwed up!" I twisted and kicked ... whoa, was she strong! She hung on.

"Listen to me!" she yelled. I slumped back onto the gravel and lay there trying to think. "You can't do it ... you can't!"

Who is this psycho? Where's Olivia the loner?

Olivia hiccupped and gulped. Two cars slowed down and the drivers stared. Then they sped up again.

I kicked hard and she lurched, throwing both arms around my calves. "Let go of me. Leave me alone!" I felt my groin muscle straining. I could drag her through the gravel, maybe a little ways – but I couldn't run away unless I kicked the bones out of her. How could this skinny little thing be so strong? Why was she doing this?

She sobbed into the tangle of her elbows and my knees, her glasses twisted up crooked on the side of her head. I grabbed her braid and pulled. "You don't know anything, you nutcase!" I screamed. "You don't know why I'm leaving. I have to go!"

A car pulled up with two women in it. One leaned out the window to watch me wailing my eyes out. "Are you hurt? Do you need help?"

That shut me up. I thought – *Yes I'm hurt. Yes I need help, you idiot!* – But what was the point.

"We're fine," I sputtered, letting the braid go. "We're talking." She stared with a look of disbelief at bawling Olivia wrapped around my legs. The women whispered to each other for a minute, stared some more, then drove slowly off.

How I can get rid of her?

Act calm. Make a joke.

"We're *fine*, aren't we," I mocked. "Aren't we fine, Olivia?"

Olivia said nothing. She just hiccupped.

I croaked, "Olivia … I have to leave. I can't go home."

No answer. "Really, listen, I can't. My dad hates me. They're all better off without me. Kids run away from home all the time. And they start life over."

I'll go someplace where I'll never have to see the disappointment on my parents' faces again.

"I'll get a job. Hey … Hans Christian Andersen – you know him. He ran away when he was 12 – and look how he turned out! And a lot of other famous people – ones I can't think of right now. Like movie stars and probably presidents … like Abraham Lincoln. Didn't he run away?"

Olivia looked up. Her face was a beety snotty mess. "Your father doesn't hate you."

"How would you know? Olivia, sorry, but you don't notice anybody with less than four legs. I really can't believe you about *my* dad."

Her face crumpled again. She gripped me tighter.

"Let go and we'll talk," I said. *Then I'll run, before I start to like the feel of her hanging onto me and not letting go.*

"It's okay. You don't need to worry about me."

"*No.* I'm not letting go." She was hiccupping again.

What's with her? She's friggin' crazy. But she can't stop me from leaving. If I don't go now, I'll go later. She's not my keeper. Just distract her.

"Why are you here? I don't get it. Why follow me?"

Olivia rolled onto her side so she could face up toward me. She pulled her glasses around, over both ears. Her face was wet and splotchy. "You brought your backpack for orienteering. You never bring it outside.

"Then I saw ... through my binoculars. You with the doll ... saying goodbye..." I felt sick.

"I saw you set a course. I thought you might run away."

"Why do you care?"

Tears ran down her face and dripped off her chin. "You tried to help me at the lake. When you thought I was drowning. I think you're more like me than anyone else...."

"I don't think so," I said. I'm not going to talk about the doll. No way.

"Whatever. I know I'm a nerd and usually it's okay. I don't care what you think. You can't go."

"Look, Olivia. You don't know anything about my home and I don't know anything about yours." By the end of the sentence, I'd stopped believing it. I remembered that she and her mother hardly looked at each other or said anything when she got picked up.

"My parents think I'm a weirdo loner who talks to trees," she said calmly. Just one hiccup. "Your parents think you're weird."

"So? I'm still leaving."

"Don't … it's too dangerous."

"It's dangerous at home."

"Your parents aren't kicking you out, are they?"

"Not exactly. Sort of."

"Then you can go back."

"Or I could leave."

She groaned like she was hurt. "Don't. It's too dangerous." I shrugged and slowly tugged one leg. She gripped harder.

"My cousin Cassandra disappeared last year," Olivia whispered, looking at my sneaker. "She was living with us, 'cause she argued with her parents. She told her friends that she was going to New York to be a model. She just disappeared."

Shivers crept down my spine. "That's terrible," I said.

"She never called her best friend like she promised to. Everybody thinks she's dead. Her parents were insane. My mom too."

Why is Olivia telling me this?

"The police came to talk to me. But that day... I didn't notice her after we got off the bus. The police thought I must have seen *something.* But I didn't."

She rubbed her wet face on her arms.

"Did some guy drive by and pick her up?" Her words came out in garbled sobs. "And I never even noticed him?"

"Olivia ...."

"My mother keeps asking and asking. She thinks I would have seen *something* ... if I wasn't such a loser."

"Liv... stop it."

"I didn't see anything!" Olivia wailed into my leg. "I didn't! I just wanted to get home... to feed my spider."

"Liv... come on. It's not your fault. Really." My legs, pressed against her body, jerked every time she sobbed.

She buried her face into her shoulder. "I wasn't trying to hurt anybody. I wasn't."

Poor Olivia. She really thought it was her fault. I didn't know what to say. She was hurting bad.

I almost patted her head. "Sorry Liv. I'm sorry."

She gulped and sobbed until she was cried out, with me staying as still as I could, clutched in her arms. Then she wiped her face on her shirt. "When I saw you put that doll in the tree, I felt … just crazy scared."

I covered my face with my hands. "Can we stop talking about it?"

"Don't go. When you get older, then do what you want. You can leave."

Tears filled my eyes again. "It's too hard." I told her. "I can't take it."

"Todd… stay. Not for your parents. 'Cause of worse people … things that could happen to you."

I lay back in the dirt with my arm over my face. This was crazy. Me here with Olivia… telling Olivia. Never in a million years would I imagine it could be like this – us two talking this way. I thought of Dad's scowl and the batting cage and sports camp coming up and more Brads everywhere watching how I talk, how I move my hips. Calling me names. I thought of riding in that car full of teenaged boys, and nights alone in the woods, and a city full of people who don't care what happens to you.

I felt Olivia wrapped around my legs like a boa constrictor.

"Please, please don't go," she whispered.

I thought of Olivia crying over the lost girl. Hating herself for not saving Cassandra, and Olivia's mother looking … accusing.

"What about you? What will you do?" I asked.

"Maybe Twig will help me … get a scholarship. I'm going to be an entomologist … or archeoastronomer."

"I don't even know what those are."

"Study insects or study what people believed about the stars in ancient times."

"Like in Greece," I said.

"And the Mayans, and the Chinese, and at Stonehenge."

She is amazing.

"Liv, my legs are numb. Can I please have them back?"

She slowly unwound her body from my legs. I bit my lip as prickles jabbed my dead feet. I stretched my legs out slowly and wiggled my ankles. Olivia sat up and stretched her shoulders this way and that, her hands resting lightly on my ankle.

This was my chance. Jerk away, push her over, run across the road ahead of that line of cars, and dash into the woods.

I wanted to, and I didn't want to. If I left, she would worry about me. And she'd be alone.

"You're right, Liv. You're more like me than anyone else at camp."

A police car slowed down and pulled over. The cop stepped out. "Todd and Olivia?"

We nodded.

"Let's go," he ordered. "Everyone's looking for you."

Maybe I'm not running away … today. That doesn't mean I want to go back.

Chapter Eleven

"Perez?" The cop said into his car radio. "I've got the two kids with me now. Winslow and Adonakis."

From the speaker came mumbles and then a long scary scream … '*AAAAIIIIIIHHHH!*' I about jumped out of my skin. The cop looked back at us, eyebrows raised. "Somebody's going to be glad to see you," he said to us, and into the radio, "Yeah, they're okay."

"That's my mother," Olivia whispered, hugging herself. She turned away from me, toward the window. A smell like wet leaves drifted my way.

I looked out my window. This hilly part of the road has changed a lot. There used to be a farm here where we came to buy pumpkins and honey when I was little. No more farm. Now the mansions were like ugly heads popping out all over the land.

"We're okay," I reminded Olivia. "We just got lost. She'll understand." Olivia didn't answer. Her hair was a mess – the braid half undone and clumps of hair sticking out. I touched her arm. "Maybe fix your braid before we get there."

"Yeah." She pulled out the elastic and combed her fingers through the long dusty hair. I picked out the leaves and twigs for her. Then I ruffled my own hair and brushed sand and dirt off my pants. I smelled funky – worse than Olivia.

We pulled into the camp driveway. "Sorry we got lost," I said to the cop. I patted Olivia gently. Finally she looked me in the eyes and nodded.

My parents stood in the driveway – Dad with his arms crossed like the Secret Service. As I got out of the cop car Mom hurried over. "Look at your legs – all scratched up!" She hugged me. Dad peered right through my skin. On the bench at the far side of the parking lot Olivia's dad had both arms wrapped around her mom, who was rocking and moaning. Olivia walked over to stand by them. Did they even notice her?

Twig appeared beside me, his face long and lined like an old man's. He squeezed my shoulder. "There you be, safe as in God's pocket." He nodded to my parents and walked over to Olivia's family.

We got into the car and rolled away.

"You really know how to worry us," Dad said, glancing at me in the rearview mirror. "Let's hear what happened."

"I ... we got lost, that's all. Went the wrong way in the woods."

Mom twisted around to look at me. "Tell us from the beginning."

I groaned. "I'm really tired."

She frowned. "Todd, tell us *something.* The police were getting organized to search the woods. You don't realize all the people involved. Twig was beside himself – flying around calling in other forest rangers."

"Well ... I guess I was using the compass wrong."

"And the girl – Olivia?" Mom said. "What about her? Were you together the whole time?"

"Mmmmm ... we got separated for awhile and then we found each other."

"I'm not happy with the lack of supervision at that camp. They need more counselors. You two should never have been out of sight."

"What were you trying to do? Run away?" Dad barked.

"No."

"Because that would be a stupid thing to do. You can't run away from problems. You have to tackle them."

"Oh, Darren. Why would he run away?"

"He looked downright depressed when the cop brought him in."

Mom gave me a pleading look. "Todd, I noticed that, too."

"Not because I was running away. It's because … I … I'm worried about Olivia," I said.

Mom jumped on that. "Oh, I know. Her mother was nearly hysterical. Rushing around yelling 'Cassandra!' So distressing! Is that Olivia's other name?"

"The woman *was* hysterical," Dad chimed in. "And completely useless. That poor husband just barely kept her from attacking Twig."

Jeez. Poor Olivia.

"What's with that family?" Dad asked.

Maybe it's not a secret. But I wasn't spilling everything Olivia told me. "Last week Brad said some weird thing happened to that family. I don't know what. Her mom gets upset a lot. And takes it out on Olivia."

"She's a strange little thing," Mom murmured. "I wonder what did happen. Poor woman. Poor girl."

We were better off talking about her family than about our own.

On the way home we stopped to pick up Casey. "Don't tell her anything," Mom warned us as she climbed out. "No need to upset her, too."

Home again. The same old walls closing in like the vines strangling the forest. What do I do now? What do I do tomorrow, and the day after that?

Dad went to read his e-mail. I was glad. But … talk about not facing your problems!

Casey came to me holding up her Go Fish cards and looking hopeful. "Sorry, Casey," I said. "I'm not playing with you right now." As I lay on my bed I felt the burn of the thorns on my legs. And the gravel from the road, working its way through my clothes, under my skin, into my throat. I wadded myself up in a ball. Pressed my hand to my mouth to keep from yelling.

Everything ahead of me looks grey and painful.

Finally I crept into the guest room and scrolled back through the caller ID, back through last week's calls until I saw 'Adonakis, Paul.' I dialed. After a long time a man answered. "Could I speak to Olivia, please?" I croaked. He sighed. "It's not convenient for her to come to the phone right now," he said, and hung up.

Oh, man. What is going down over there? I went back to my room, sat and thumbed through the books on my shelf. Nothing I wanted to read. I wished I had a Fairytopia story … Layla, Flora, and Bloom to fly in and cheer me up.

"Todd! Telephone!" Mom yelled.

It was Olivia. "Did you call me?" she asked.

"Yeah."

"I guessed it was you. My father didn't want me to talk, for some reason."

Her voice was so low I had to jam my palm over my other ear. "How are you doing?" I asked.

"My mother is upset. Dad is with her."

"Are they mad at you?"

"Yes. There's nothing I can do. Just wait for her to get over it. But what about you?"

"It's the same as before. Not better. Dad guessed that I wanted to run away. It should have been obvious, because ... well, because of some stuff going on here. I said no, we just got lost."

"But... they're glad you are back. I know they are. I saw your mom hug you."

"Yeah, yeah."

"Better to be home than out in the woods tonight. Isn't it?"

She didn't sound very happy to be where she was, either. I looked out the window. It was dark. "I don't know...I think it's not going to work for me to be at home."

Silence. I wished I could tell her ... everything.

"Isn't tomorrow the last day of camp?" she said finally.

"That's right, it is. I lost track. Oh, great."

"What do you mean?"

"The last day of camp means I'm about to begin sports camp."

She groaned. "Sorry." She was making an effort to talk.

"So I'll see you tomorrow," I said.

"If my parents let me come to camp." She sounded bad.

"Try to come. Seriously. ... Are you sure you're okay?"

Her voice skipped over the words. "Mom doesn't understand why I would hurt her so."

"Liv! That's not fair. You weren't trying to hurt her."

I heard her sniffle. "I should know she can't handle me being missing."

"Liv... you told her we just got lost, right?"

"Yes."

"You should ... tell her *I* got lost and you found me. Or tell her the truth... so she won't blame *you.*"

"She didn't even come and talk to me about it. She just went to her room and closed herself away."

"Like my dad went off to his computer. Please tell your mom that you stopped me from running away. Or I'll tell her." My chest clutched, thinking how this could get back to my parents. What the heck. "Liv, ask her to come to the phone."

"You're a good person," she whispered. "But when she's like this ... I'm afraid of what she might say to you. But thank you."

I tried to think what I could do.

"You're not mad at me anymore? About stopping you from hitchhiking?" Her voice was high and tight.

I got a lump in my throat remembering her clutching my legs, tears running down her face.

"No, I'm not mad."

* * * * *

The last morning of camp turned out okay. We played crazy nature charades. Twig had us in hysterics, lumbering around with his tongue flicking out pretending to be an anteater. But he and I were the only ones who got a kick out of Olivia impersonating a sponge. Then we had to clear away all our projects and clean up.

"So which one of you got lost first? Why didn't you just follow the trails back here?" Sylvie grilled Olivia as they mopped the tables. "There are blazes everywhere! …Or did you put another spell on Todd? What were you two doing together in the woods, anyway?"

Olivia glared at her and walked away.

"Come on, Sylvie," I said. "She's not that bad. Just a little different."

Sylvie giggled. "Like Chucky is just a little different. A little freaky and completely psycho."

"What's the big deal? She's quiet. She's going to be a scientist… an astronomer or something. She knows … a lot. She's just not that comfortable with people."

"A *scientist*," Sylvie sneered. "You have got to be kidding. But ...really, why was she following you?"

"I guess she takes the buddy system very seriously." I grinned at her, but she snorted. "Yeah, right."

"Anyway – just leave her alone, okay?"

"You like her better than me – that bites."

Together we turned the table over to push up the legs. "Don't be a dope, Vogue. I like you too. Hey, what's happening with your family?"

Sylvie flipped another table leg in. "They're getting separated. Dad's going to Italy ... for a year. My mom's putting big pressure on me to stay with her." Sylvie looked away for a minute, biting her lip. "I know I'm a bitch, but I don't want to stay with her. It's too depressing. She won't do anything for herself. I told her she should be an interior designer – she's fabulous at designing. Dad says if I learn Italian this summer, I can go with him. I can go to the international school in Rome in the fall. But he wants me to know the language. That's cool. I'm signing up for an intensive class – a whole year of Italian in two months. But my mom..."

"Maybe she will find something too... if there are no kids at home."

Sylvie brightened up. "That's right. She always said she couldn't go back to decorating because she wanted to take care of her own house. But she stopped going out, and dropped all her friends.

Blamed my father, but he never held her back. I'm going to sit her down to search all the design schools and make her pick one, like Dad got the language course information for me. It'll be better for her to be busy. And when Christmas comes she'll fly over so we can all be together."

"Hey, come on," interrupted Brad. Olivia was behind him. "Twig wants us to go down to the pond and bring up the equipment."

We followed him out the door. "Twig says if we don't all stay together he'll have our heads." He thrust his thermos at Sylvie. "Try my own mixture of Seven-Up and fruit juice."

One last day with Brad. Then I never have to see him again.

She tipped up the built-in straw. "I'm so thirsty!"

"Don't gulp it so fast – you'll get gas," he told her. I was thirsty, too, but he didn't offer it to me. Whatever.

"I can't believe camp is over," Sylvie said, pouting.

Brad leaned toward her. "Don't worry Vogue. You and I will chill. Starting tonight?" He glanced at me. "*Maybe* Winzo too. But he's better off lost."

Sylvie kept gulping from Brad's thermos as we sauntered down the hill. There was the pond – peaceful dark water with its fringe of green grasses. A couple of bullfrogs harrumphed.

"It's so nice here!" Sylvie spun around waving her head. "But I'm dizzy!" she laughed and thumped down into the grass. Brad sat beside her. Olivia and I kept walking along the bank gathering up the buckets and nets and collection boxes. When I looked back, Brad was pulling Sylvie onto his lap and whispering in her ear. I heard her giggle. Olivia stared at them.

"Something's going on," she said, frowning.

"I guess they were bound to hook up sooner or later," I said. I wanted to ask Olivia if we would see each other again, but I didn't want to sound … dorky. So I kept going around the pond, the sun stroking my cheek. Feeling pretty good. I survived the Brad plague – barely. Maybe I can fool people. I can be someone else – when I need to. And in eighth grade, I'll need to.

We're all changing. Olivia looks different. Maybe she washed her hair.

Brad has some hair on his face. He'll be shaving soon.

I'm changing too. I have dark brown hair on my legs. My pits smell. I can't believe I'm going to be a man. But I have to. Once you change, you can't go back. Like the butterfly never goes back to being a caterpillar. And the frog can't ever be a tadpole again. Only in magic and movies can you go back and forth. When you make up your own story, anything can happen.

If I could make up the ending of the Little Mermaid story, she'd be able to switch back and forth. When she dove into the water, her tail would suddenly appear. And when she climbed out, she'd have legs. And the prince and all their friends could do the same, so they could go visit her family under the sea whenever they wanted. That would be the perfect ending.

Olivia looked back again. Brad and Sylvie were making out.

"Why is Sylvie acting so different?" Olivia asked.

It *was* kind of strange. "Well, it's the last day."

We circled the pond and reached them. Sylvie had her arms wound around Brad. She threw back her head. "I'm still dizzy!"

"She's drunk," Olivia whispered into my ear.

"Brad!" I yelled. "What was in that thermos?" He chuckled. I grabbed it off the ground, unscrewed the top, and sniffed. Weird smell. Olivia sniffed. We shrugged at each other. I poured the last drops into the grass.

"Brad! You'll get her in trouble!" I pulled Sylvie's arm. "Sylvie, get up, you're drunk."

Brad grinned at us. "She'll be okay – there wasn't much…"

"Why did you do it? You ever think of anybody but yourself?!" I yelled. "What if …she fell and hurt herself … like Foster did?"

Brad looked at me knowingly and laughed. "I'd take better care of her …"

I gulped. "Better than you took care of *Foster*? I knew you messed with that arrow … you lied to us! You pointed it the wrong way and Foster followed it, didn't he … and he fell through the rotten bridge."

Brad gave Sylvie a kiss and muttered into her neck, "I didn't know he was so blind he'd fall in …"

"You lie so bad! Let go of Sylvie."

"What are you going to do about it?" I kicked him in the side, as hard as I could .

"Ow!" he bellowed. I grabbed Sylvie and pulled her away. Olivia came to help her stand up. Brad staggered up and grabbed me around the neck. "You're mine, Dude!" We fell on the ground. He slugged me in the face. Sylvie and Olivia started screaming. I tasted blood. Tried to block his fists. Olivia wrapped herself around one of his arms, and Sylvie fell across his chest. I dove for his legs.

"Unnnhh! Get off me!" he yelled, thrashing around. We hung on.

"It's over, Brad! Quit it or I tell Twig everything!"

"You little fag!" he grunted.

"Shut up," I said. "It's over!"

He swore at us, but he stopped fighting. Olivia and I helped Sylvie up. "We'll take Sylvie – you get the stuff," I told Brad. "Just *do it.*"

I must be out of my mind.

I never would have kicked him if Olivia and Sylvie hadn't been involved.

Sylvie's head bobbled around in circles. "I have noooo idea what just happened! Who started it?"

"Brad did," I said, my voice still shaky.

Olivia and I hobbled to the trail, Sylvie propped up between us. "Just try to act normal when we get back to camp, Sylvie. Brad put alcohol in that juice."

We left him sprawled on the grass, glaring.

Chapter Twelve

When I woke up Saturday morning the phone was ringing.

So camp was over. No more Brad. He can fall into a hole for all I care. Get swiped by aliens – even better. And maybe no more Sylvie? But she asked for my email address, and said she'll teach me some Italian.

At least Boxo is free. Yesterday while everyone was busy saying goodbye to Twig, I slipped into the Discovery Room and lifted Boxo out of his tank, hid him under my shirt, and hustled out to the butterfly garden. I put Boxo way back under the big bushes. He'll dig for worms in the soil and watch the butterflies flutter from flower to flower. Or he can mosey back into the woods and eat wild raspberries.

The phone rang again. If it's Olivia, I want to talk to her. But probably not. She's not a big phone person.

I climbed out of bed and went downstairs to see what was up.

My parents were arguing in the kitchen. I skidded to a halt to listen outside the door. Dad was sputtering

"Today? An appointment *today?*"

"Yes. At noon," Mom said. "We need to wake up Casey and Todd."

"You called a psychologist without telling me? Who, Bert Mathews? Listen, I'm not going to spill my guts to old Bert. I do business with his wife. No way."

"We're not going to Bert Mathews. We're going into the District."

"All the way down to D.C.?"

"Yes, to somebody we don't know. His office is off Dupont Circle," Mom said.

Dad scowled. "Why did you just drop this on me?"

"We need help. You know it and I know it. Everybody in this house is angry. We can't go on this way. I found a family therapist who has experience with this … with what's going on here. I talked with him a few days ago."

"What do you mean? Experience with what?" Dad said.

"With boys who are … different. Helping the boys and their families," Mom said.

"You didn't discuss it with *me*!" Dad yelped.

They didn't discuss it with me either. They can't make me go!

"If you're right about Todd wanting to run away ... don't you see?" Mom pleaded. "We need help even more!"

"Maybe I was wrong. I don't know where that came from. He probably just got lost. But why didn't you ask me about this psychologist appointment?"

"Dr. Montoya just called me this minute. Somebody cancelled for today, so he has time for us. Otherwise, we wait a month. Darren, we have to go. We have to start talking. I can't stand it any more. We can't wait a whole month!"

"How is some stranger going to help us? He doesn't know anything about us."

"He learns about us. That's his job."

If Dad doesn't go, I won't have to go.

Dad grumbled. "He should talk to Todd. He's got the problem. Warn him what's in store for him if he doesn't shape up. I don't need to talk to the guy."

"No, we're all going. And he wants to meet Casey."

"Casey?"

"Yes," Mom said.

Dad groaned. "I don't see why."

I don't know if I want Casey there or not. How much protection can I get from a five-year-old?

I walked into the kitchen. "If you make me go I'm not going to talk," I said.

They both glared at me.

Dad settled back in the chair and cleared his throat. "Todd, there are issues here that you need to deal with. You can't hide from them."

At that, Mom raised her eyebrows, but Dad didn't look at her.

"You need to get some perspective from another adult," Dad went on, nodding and rubbing his chin like a wise man. "You don't realize the … uh … consequences of your behavior. Other people could make life difficult for you."

So this guy is supposed to 'fix' me.

I just said, "Everything's fine. You two don't need to worry."

"But we do worry," Mom said.

She's trying. She really is.

"I know *you* worry," I said to her. "A couple of nights ago I heard you crying, Mom."

Mom looked confused. Then the frown cleared. She turned to Dad. "Darren, please go up and wake Casey."

Dad grunted, glanced quickly at both of us, then he got up and left.

Mom turned to me with a soft look. "Two nights ago?" she said. "Todd … that wasn't *me* crying."

I felt shivers down my arms.

Dad.

Dad cried over me.

* * * * *

Two hours later we were in D.C. traffic.

In the car Dad handed me the daily practice schedule for that sports camp I'm going to on Monday. I was *so* grateful to be reminded.

But I couldn't figure out – why did Dad cry about me?

"I knew parking would be impossible down here," Dad said, turning into another street packed with cars.

"We still have fifteen minutes," Mom said

I'm in no hurry. This doctor will pressure me to explain about the skirt. What do I say? That I was fumbling in my closet for my pajamas and put it on by mistake, in the dark? Right. Or that it was a joke, like the comics on TV? I'm dead either way.

"There's one! On the other side!" Mom called out.

"Hang on … I'm doing a U-ie!"

Dad flung us across the seat with his U-turn. The brakes squealed. We jolted backward, into the space.

"Finally! Good thing we left early," Mom said. "What's this … 20th? We're four blocks away. We need to get over to 16th Street."

"Come on, kids!" Dad said. We clambered out.

Casey doesn't realize what she's in for. She's happy to be going somewhere with the family. She brought a Barbie along to meet the man we are going to talk to. That's just about funny.

Imagine me saying, "Oh, yeah. I stole a Barbie. She was hidden in my room for two weeks."

"Hustle!" Dad urged, leading the way down the street.

The street was getting crowded. Groups of people were all walking the same direction we were going. I could hear whistles and cheers in the distance. People around me looked happy, like they were expecting something.

"Maybe it's a street fair," Mom said. "This is why it's fun to come into the District. There's always something going on."

"Can we go, Daddy?" Casey pleaded. "Please!"

"Maybe after our meeting, honey," Dad said.

I hadn't been to D.C. for months, not since we went to the new IMAX at the Air and Space Museum. It was so different to be in a crowded street with restaurants and stores and people all around. I wished I could explore.

A crowd was standing at the next corner, not moving. When we got there, I saw the whole street was lined with people on both sides. A policeman was stringing a yellow "Police Line – Do Not Cross" ribbon across the street.

"Woooo! Yea!" People cheered and whistled.

Over the heads of the crowd I caught glimpses of fancy costumes in the middle of the street – crowns, feathers, shiny turbans.

Casey pointed. "Mommy! A parade!"

I squeezed past someone to peek onto the street. Wow.

Two women strolled by arm in arm, in fancy gowns. One had long blond hair down her back and a tight scarlet gown to her ankles. The other had long black hair and a shining silver dress, slit way up her leg. They wore mile-high platform heels – transparent and covered with spangles.

"Shake it girl!" somebody called out.

Behind them came more ladies – in tight black low-cut dresses – then one in short leather shorts and a vest tight over her breasts. Then two Asian women in flowing white gauzy dresses with huge long sleeves. The sleeves reached the ground and the women waved them in circles like banners. They looked up shyly under their long eyelashes as people cheered.

What kind of parade was this? Nobody marching in formation. All the women in little groups, just walking along.

"I can't see, Daddy!" Casey complained.

"I'll pick you up, honey. Let's get across the street first. We have to keep going."

"Come on," a guy next to me said to his friend. "Let's get down to the finish line." They hurried off.

Finish line?

I stopped for two airline hostesses pulling luggage behind them. They had really big hair. Maybe those are wigs. I could barely see their faces through all their make-up.

"Where are you flying, ladies?' a young woman next to me said.

The blonde with big curly hair pouted her shiny red lips. "Coffee, tea, or…."

Her voice was low, like a man's.

She turned to me and winked. Her partner gave me a little wave. They were men. I think.

They were men.

The two stewardesses wiggled their hips and walked on down the street.

"Happy skies, girls!" a man called out.

People came out of the cafes behind us, holding their coffees and drinks. Some were standing up on chairs to see over the crowd. And across the street people leaned out of the second story windows. Everybody looked happy.

It was like a crazy movie.

A big heavy woman … or maybe a man, dressed in a long purple gown and a headdress of swirling purple snakes, tossed silver beads to us.

"Celebrate!" she croaked in a high fake voice.

She's a man too. *I don't believe this.*

I saw Dad crossing the street in a crowd with Mom and Casey. He was looking around. "Todd!" he yelled.

Then two police cars pulled up behind the crowd, cutting Dad off from my side of the street.

"Okay, folks, please keep back behind the white line," the cop said through his loudspeaker. "Please do not cross the street. The main event is about to begin." But Mom and Dad and Casey had already crossed over.

I had to see more. I *had* to.

I slipped around the side of a parked car and crouched down by the front fender.

A beautiful dark-skinned woman in a bright blue ballet tutu danced by, throwing handfuls of candy to the crowd. I grabbed a green one. Other people were eating them, so I did too. Mmmm.... Lime.

Then a redheaded woman in a pink smock came over and handed out tiny lipsticks to the couple next to me. "I see you in a page boy, honey, and a green silk frock – with a V-neck. You know, the V-neck is flattering to the full figure," she said in a man's voice to the young guy near me.

The guy and his girlfriend and their buddies all laughed along. "Okay, thanks," he said. "I'll keep that in mind."

"Princess Diana!" someone yelled. A beautiful woman with smooth blond hair and a pink suit walked by escorted by two men wearing sunglasses, like bodyguards. She blew kisses to the crowd.

"Your highness!" people called out.

I looked across to the other side. Dad stood in the street arguing with a policeman and pointing toward my side of the street. The policeman motioned Dad to get back to the curb. Dad looked upset.

But I'm staying here. Just a little longer!

"Bystanders keep back, Please! The race is about to begin!" the loudspeaker blared.

Will Dad and Mom notice who these people really are? Good grief, Dad freaked out with my measly little skirt. He's gonna have a heart attack!

Should I go over and try to get them away from here before they find out?

A blond teenager in a crop top and hip huggers came close to me. She looked just like Christina Aquilera.

"Great makeover, Christina!" The boy beside me said. "Good luck in the race!" She nodded to him and smiled and strutted off.

I can't tell. Honest. I can't tell if that was a girl or a boy.

"Didn't she … I mean he … win last year?" the guy beside me said to his girlfriend. He saw me looking up at him.

"Amazing, huh?" he said, grinning at me.

"Is that a man?" I asked him. *It can't be.*

"They're *all* men," he said, widening his eyes. "It's the high heel race!"

They're *men*. Out here in the street. In front of everybody.

"The church ladies!" a woman near me cheered.

Three gray-wigged women, or I guess men, in droopy cardigan sweaters and faded housedresses shuffled by in fuzzy slippers. One had a sign saying "Jesus loves you… in that outfit!" The crowd loved it.

How could they do this? How could they dare??

I looked into the faces of the men dressed as women. Some looked serious – like the airline hostesses and Princess Diana and the pouty ladies in party gowns – like actors playing their parts. Some were giggling with each other and talking to people in the crowd. The church ladies were chattering together like mice.

Then I saw long red-orange hair. A long strapless green dress, ending in a tail. A zippered opening showing bright green heels. Green gloves above the elbow. A sequined purse shaped like a fish.

The Little Mermaid. Tall and proud. Right here in the street. She can be anything she wants. Just the way I imagined.

"Todd! Todd!" Dad was directly across the street, yelling at me. "Stay right there! I'm coming!"

He found me.

Christina Aquilera walked by Dad. A newsman with a TV camera on his shoulder stopped to film her. Dad stepped back dazed, horrified.

He ran across the street to me.

"Todd!" he said. "This is … uh … this is …"

"I know," I said.

The same policeman walked up to Dad. "You're not going to try that again, are you?" he asked Dad.

"I found my son. He's right here. I want to get him out of here."

"Sit tight. The race is beginning. It'll be over in 30 seconds," the policeman said.

"What kind of weird show is this?" Dad asked him.

The policeman laughed. "It's your first time?"

"Hey, it was unintentional. We got stuck in it," Dad said angrily.

"It's the yearly cross-dress high heel race," the cop said … as if it was totally normal, like a school Field Day. Dad stared at him.

A cow-person in big spotted dress and a horned hat stopped beside us. "What am I? What am I?"

"Bessie the Cow?" someone in the crowd yelled.

The cow-lady flapped her huge eyelashes and gave us a silly grin. "The Dairy Queen, of course," she said.

"Hey, Brett!" the policeman said to the cow-lady. She looked at him.

"Hey, John!" she said in a low voice.

"Hope we'll see you this week. It's freezing up on me again."

The cow nodded. "I'm coming over on Thursday."

"Good luck!" the cop yelled as the cow hurried down to the ribbon where everyone was lining up.

Dad and I stared at the cop. "You know that ... um ...," Dad stammered.

"Oh, sure," the cop said. "Brett is our computer genius. He's over at the precinct every month, working out our computer kinks. He's a great guy – donates a lot of time."

Dad stared at the cop like he might be from outer space.

The cop laughed again. "He *doesn't* wear the cow suit to work."

POW! The starting gun!

The crowd of runners burst through the ribbon and clattered toward us. A princess in a tall white wig tripped splat! onto the road. Everyone else raced by – prom gowns, tutus, leather pants, nightgowns. The mermaid ran in huge strides, her tail unzipped all the way up and clenched in her hand.

The princess staggered to her feet, shoved her wig up onto her head, lifted her huge hooped skirts, and trotted past.

The cheers swept over us in a wave following the runners up the street. I glanced at Dad. He looked amazed. He leaned out to see who was winning. We couldn't see the finish line.

I heard cheers for the winner. It was over. The crowd around us broke up and emptied into the street, heading off in all directions.

Nothing like this has ever happened to me before.

My teeth were chattering. It was a hot day, but I was shaking.

Those men aren't afraid. They aren't afraid! And nobody cared what they wore.

Dad stood there looking stunned.

I would never do it. I'd be too embarrassed, in front of all those people. Wouldn't wear all that make-up. And I'd kill myself on those spike heels.

I looked at Dad. He still looked lost.

But the men here dressed up, because they felt like it. And everybody loved it.

Do their parents come? *What about their parents?*

I guess it doesn't matter any more what their parents think. They aren't afraid.

Then Dad looked into my eyes. *He'll see my heart jumping!*

I can't help it.

Dad looked surprised. As if he hadn't looked at his son for a long time.

I reached out and took his elbow. "Come on. Let's go find Mom."

I led him across the street, through the crowd.

Mom and Casey were waving to us from the next corner.

"There they are, Dad."

Chapter Thirteen

I've never been so tired. We were in that office about three hours.

"Why didn't he talk to *me*?" Casey pouted as we walked back to the car.

"Dr. Montoya did come out to the waiting room and meet you," Mom answered.

"But I didn't get to go inside. Todd did," Casey said.

"Be glad you didn't. It wasn't that fun," I said.

Purple and gold necklaces and green candy from the high-heel race lay in the gutter here and there. Casey bent over to pick up a gold necklace.

Mom reached out to pull her arm away. "Don't, Casey. They're dirty," she said, glancing at me. I had a purple one hidden in my pocket.

Did Mom and Dad tell Dr. Montoya about the high-heel race? And why are they so quiet?

When we met Dr. Montoya, he said he'd talk to our parents first. Casey and I stayed in the waiting room while they talked a long time. Probably telling him about the skirt and how all wrong their son is.

As we drove out of the city I asked, "I don't have to go back there, do I?"

"Yes," Mom said. "We're going back."

"Why? Why do I have to go back?"

"Because," she insisted.

"I'm not sure I'm going back," Dad said.

"Oh, *Darren*," Mom groaned.

"I said I'd come once," he went on. "That doesn't mean I'm going to roll over and do everything the guy asks me to do. What if he's wrong and I'm right?"

Good old Dad.

In the waiting room I read a book called "*The Sissy Duckling*" while Casey was looking at the toys. The book was about a little duck who got called a sissy. When the flock was flying south, his dad got shot by a hunter. The little duck stayed behind and the two of them were stuck all winter in the cold north. They only survived because the little duck knew all about cooking and nursing and keeping a house warm. Then his dad loved him.

I should buy that book for Dad.

When Mom and Dad finally came out of the office, I had to go in by myself.

This Dr. Montoya had a playroom for an office. He had dolls and a dollhouse, cars and trucks and fire engines. He had checkers and board games and boxes of markers and crayons. He even had a sandbox up on legs, like a table. And there were black-haired and red-haired mermaids sitting on the sand.

He said I could look at any of the toys, but I didn't touch anything.

We sat down to talk. That was the worst part.

I thought he'd tell me I had to shape up. I thought he'd say it's really bad for a boy my age to ever want to dress up or play with mermaids. I thought he'd say grow up, you're ruining your life. You're ruining your parents' lives.

But he didn't say that at all.

At first I didn't hear much. I was too scared.

He said it's rough when boys like things that most other boys don't like. It's the same for girls. I don't need to feel ashamed of it. There's nothing wrong with it, he said, but it's rough. I probably get lonely a lot, he said, and don't think I'll ever have a real friend –who is a boy like me.

Then Dr. Montoya told me about boys he's known who liked beautiful things and flowers and fabrics. He talks to boys every week who sometimes imagine they are fairies or mermaids and might like to dress up. They like other stuff too – hip-hop, or computers, or math. He said these boys, who he knows personally, grew up to be teachers or pilots or video-game designers, or anything they wanted to be.

And they're fine. There's nothing wrong with them.

He said he knows there are sometimes bullies who hate you for no reason, but that it will get better. He said when I grow up it won't be so rough because I'll meet other people who like the things I like and I'll have lots of friends.

There are all kinds of ways of being a boy, he said.

I wouldn't believe him if I hadn't seen that race.

He understands how hard it is to keep going when no one believes in you and there's not one person you can tell.

So I told him. *A lot.*

* * * * *

Dad took our exit off the Beltway and headed north toward home. The roads were crammed with Saturday shoppers.

"Dr. Montoya said we could each ask for something from the rest of the family," Mom said.

"Nobody yelling," Casey piped up.

"I want my family to stop treating me like the bad guy." Dad muttered.

"What I want is for us to come to counseling until Dr. Montoya says we don't need to come anymore," Mom said firmly.

After a minute Dad said, "Todd?"

"I don't want to go to sports camp," I said.

"What *do* you want to do?" he asked.

"Take a dive off the ten-meter platform," I said, on a whim.

"Diving isn't a sport," Dad said.

I had him then. "It's an Olympic sport, Dad."

"So is sliding downhill on a sled," Dad scoffed. "And pushing stones across the ice. Luge and curling. Both Olympic sports."

"*Darren*," Mom said, staring hard at him. "Dr. Montoya said that Todd will only do well at something *he* wants to do, not the things *we* want him to do."

"Which platform did you say? *Ten meters*? Just where are you going to find a ten-meter platform?" Dad asked.

"I know where," I said. *I'm taking you on, Dad. And I'm calling the pool when I get home.*

Mom gasped. "Ten meters! That's thirty feet up in the air! I hope you're not serious."

Dad shook his head. "I'm not paying for diving lessons. You wouldn't jump from ten meters anyway."

"I'll get a job."

Dad bopped his palm against his forehead. "Oh, I completely forgot. Twig called this morning."

I sat up straight in my seat.

"He asked me if you might want a job as a counselor aide for the next session. I guess they have a big group of younger kids coming in. I told him you'd be too busy...."

"Dad!"

"*Darren.*" Mom sounded excited. She turned back to me.

"Yes, I want to! I can work at camp during the day and go to dive team at night. Call Twig when we get home. Okay?"

Mom nodded. She turned to Dad. "Why not?"

"B-but he registered for baseball camp!" Dad sputtered.

"He never wanted that. You forced him into it," Mom said.

Dad rolled his head. "I give up. Whatever."

Mom smiled at me.

Dad cleared his throat. "Oh, and that girl ... the one that got lost with you. Twig is offering her a job, too."

I grinned. Awesome. Me and Liv...and Twig ...following raccoon tracks ... finding salamanders ... teaching the kids to use a compass. Maybe I'll even see Boxo out in the butterfly garden, digging for a worm.

I let my window down and the wind blew full force into my face. Over that way, a few miles, is the camp. The pond, the shady stream, the frogs, and the dragonflies. Waiting for me.

Was it just two days since I ran away and Liv stopped me?

It felt like that happened a month ago.

I closed my eyes.

* * * * *

A boy steps onto the ten-meter platform. He looks down at the crowd. They are quiet, waiting for his last dive. If he nails it, he moves into first place.

He lifts his right arm to signal the judges that he's ready.

He rises onto his toes, strides to the edge and leaps out into space forming a perfect cross, arms outstretched, head straight and in plane with his body. He jack-knifes till his head meets his knees, pivots his legs straight behind him, and pierces the water with barely a ripple.

Underwater the Little Mermaid is waiting, her long light hair floating, arms reaching out. "Come away with me, Todd. Hurry, Captain Hook is stealing our gold! There's a passage to Wonderland. We need you!"

I squeeze her hands.

"Sorry, I can't. I'm competing. I might win this. Dad and Mom are here watching me. Tomorrow I'll come."

I dolphin-kick to the side and hoist myself up, my bare toes firm and sure on the grainy tile.

Printed in the United States
111592LV00001B/53/A

9 781598 583595